HELLO,

HONEYBEE

CAITY H

Dedication:

There are a lot of people who've encouraged me throughout this process of writing. I am very grateful to all of the people who've been here since the beginning, family, friends, and all those who read Honeybee on Inkpop.com. I've felt so blessed throughout writing Honeybee, having so much support and love.

To Carman and Kaylyn, you two have been there since the beginning, pushing me to finish the book and helping me figure out the story of Lex and Olivia. I love you both very much, and I couldn't have done it without you.

To Joanna, thank you for helping me with the cover picture and for being so excited about this book, and others. It means so much to me!

To Jelsa, and countless other Inkies, I'm very grateful to you all for helping me with the editing process. All the threats really kept me going. I've come a long way since the first draft of this book, roughly three years ago, and I have you all to thank for that.

Thank you to my mom for always being there and supporting me and my dream to be an author. I love you very much!

There are a lot of people to thank, a lot of people who read this story and helped me make it better. I am truly blessed to know so many amazing people, and I love you all.

Biggest thanks go out to my Lord and Savior, Jesus Christ, for giving me this ability.

Much love,

Table of Contents

Chapter One – Senior Year

His tall body moved through the crowd of students. A smile lit up his face, and his dazzling green eyes sparkled. Lex Diamond. With his shaggy blond hair, muscular body, and star soccer player status he was the *it* guy of Riverside High School.

His arm was wrapped around his girlfriend, Cassandra Peacock. They had been together since last summer. She was the typical skinny blonde that popular guys in movies always went after. It killed me to see them together. Ever since I was fourteen I'd pictured Lex and I falling in love one day, and becoming the "*it*" couple at school. The memory from four years ago surfaced in my head.

"What do you think about starting high school in a few weeks?" he asked.

I shrugged my shoulders. "It should be interesting." I glanced around the tree house, the picture of our families together on the Fourth of July years earlier, sitting on a small table. A prickling sensation touched my eyes when I looked at my dad, his arm wrapped around Mom and me. It still hurt to see his picture. My dad was such a big part of my life, when he died I thought I would never stop crying. Sniffing, I turned back to Lex. "It'll probably be lonely, too."

"Why is that?" he asked, raising an eyebrow.

"I didn't really have any friends in middle school, Lex. I doubt I'm going to have a better time in high school." I replied honestly.

"I'm sorry," he murmured. "I know I wasn't a very good friend to you." He grabbed my hand, rubbing his

thumb over my skin. His touch sent shivers up and down my spine.

"It's okay," I said, letting my breath out shakily.

"I think I should have my first kiss before I go into high school," he said abruptly.

"Haven't you already?" he shook his head. "Oh." My eyes looked at our hands and realized that they were intertwining. He was holding my hand. Lex Diamond was holding my hand. Lex. I felt my body temperature rising.

"Honeybee," he said, using the nickname he'd given me when we were kids. I looked up at him. I could get lost in those deep green irises. His eyes shifted to my lips.

I blinked and then it happened.

He leaned forwards, pressing his lips against mine. After the initial shock, I leaned into the kiss, letting the sensations of his lips on mine wash over me. Butterflies filled my stomach, and I felt like I could burst from the happiness pouring into my body.

After a few moments, he moved away. He leaned his forehead against mine, our noses touching. Nothing could've kept me from smiling at that moment. Things were changing.

I sighed, letting the memory fade away. After we had kissed, he didn't talk to me the rest of the summer, and ignored me at school. When he became popular, things really changed. I was no longer someone he could spend the weekend watching movies with.

"You're doing it again," Bethany Bridges mumbled, pausing in her rant about Mr. Trill's science assignment that was due next Monday.

I looked up, blonde waves swaying in front of my eyes. "What?"

"Olivia, I'm your best friend." She leaned on one hip, crossing her arms over her chest. "I know when you're checking out Lex again."

I gaped and slapped her arm. "I'm not checking him out. I'm glaring at him in secret," I corrected her.

She titled her head to the side, black hair falling over her shoulder. "Alright, what happened?"

"What always happens," I mumbled, leaning my back against the lockers. "He brings up some memory from our childhood and embarrasses me with it." He'd told them about a time we went swimming and I accidentally walked into the men's restroom and came out crying. It was a tad bit hurtful that people laughed at my childhood traumas. It hurt worse that Lex was the one telling them.

"Want me to run him over with my car?" she asked, slamming her locker shut. "Maybe I'll hit his pretty little girlfriend too!" She beamed.

I laughed, shaking my head. "No, that's not necessary. But you'll be happy to hear I stuck my tongue out at him when his back was turned."

She chuckled. "You sure showed him." We walked toward our next classes. "Good grief that man gets on my nerves." She frowned.

"I know," I murmured. The fact my heart had been wrapped up in him since I was fourteen made it easy to love him, and also incredibly easy to loathe him. It was utterly confusing.

"I bet it makes Cassy jealous," she started, glancing at me.

I raised an eyebrow in question. I wasn't Cassy, and I was pretty sure nothing about me made her jealous. I had thick blonde hair, blue eyes that required glasses, and a slim build. She was thin and busty; the boys were wrapped around her finger.

"When he calls you Honeybee," she clarified.

"Why?"

"Because!" She declared. "He doesn't have a nickname for her, and your nickname has the word 'honey' in it. I'd feel jealous if my super-hot boyfriend called a girl he didn't seem to like honey."

I smirked and glanced over at her through my glasses. "You think he's super-hot?"

She burst out laughing at me. A few students looked at us like we were a pair of orange leprechauns walking down the hallway. They had no patience for people who enjoyed having fun.

"What?"

"I do *not* think that Lex Diamond is hot!" she exclaimed loudly. "I was talking from your point of view."

I slapped her arm. "Shut up!" There were people around who did have working ears. I didn't need it getting back to him that I thought he was hot. He had enough power over me already.

"It's true!" She giggled. I dragged her into our homeroom, stopping the conversation. We sat in the second row and waited for Mrs. Bitsley to come in.

The rest of the classroom was busy texting, talking, and eating leftover lunch, but they all noticed when Lex came in. Everyone stopped their chatter as he walked through the door.

I used to get flustered when he walked into a room, hoping he would smile, or acknowledge my existence and our former friendship. Not anymore though. Now I would just turn my head, hoping he would walk by without throwing an insult.

"Honeybee, want to go swimming later?" he asked as he walked by. His sarcastic question sent the whole class into laughter. My cheeks burned bright red. He smiled and walked to the back where the rest of his friends were. The chattering soon continued, filling the classroom with noise.

Bethany glared at Lex once before turning back to me. "Ignore him. We only have a few more weeks of school and then we'll be free of him. It's highly unlikely that his soccer scholarship will get him into the schools we applied to."

I knew she was trying to make me feel better, but it almost made my heart sink farther. As rude as Lex could be, he was still one of those people I secretly wanted to become friends with again. A part of my heart still longed to be with his. I didn't like admitting it out loud, but Lex still held me prisoner. If he changed his ways I wouldn't stand a chance. I would fall into his arms faster than he could tell me he was just kidding.

"Yeah, I can't wait." The words fell from my lips with no gumption.

"Olivia," she sighed, slapping the top of my desk. "You will get over that jerk when you don't have to see him every day." I wasn't so sure. Even when we got out of school for the summer, I would still see him all the time. Living next door to him was both a privilege and a punishment. "Trust me, Livie. Things will get better in time."

"If you say so." I adjusted the clunky blue glasses that sat atop my nose. The pair of sky blue glasses had graced my face for the past couple of years. I'd lost my fire truck red glasses when Lex *accidentally* stepped on them. There was very little chance it had actually been a mistake.

Sighing, I turned my attention to the front of the room. The white board had nicks of color across its surface, missed when the teachers using it erased their notes. The

California sun streaked through the windows, the cracks and dirt shadows on the linoleum floor. The teacher's desk was at the front of the classroom, papers and pencils scattered over the top of it.

"You're still coming over to my house after school for swimming, right?" Bethany looked over to me, an expectant smile on her face.

I nodded. "Of course. What are the odds that Lex tells them my swimming pool horror today?"

She grinned, shooting a glance back at him. "He's probably stalking you and listened to our conversation last night."

I frowned at the idea. Lex didn't really strike me as the stalker type. Of course, we hadn't really talked much other than passing snide comments in the hallway. I supposed it was possible that he became a secret stalker in my absence. Maybe it was even because of me that he turned into a creeper.

I shook my head, clearing my thoughts. "No. He wouldn't waste his time outside my window when he could go make out with his girlfriend, or work out," I decided.

With a shrug of her shoulders, she pulled out her notebook. "You never know," she said. Mrs. Bitsley, our English teacher, came in and our conversation came to an end.

The sun shone down on me, my body temperature rising. I was outside the school waiting for Bethany. Since I was without a car, and we lived ten minutes away from each other, she dropped me off on her way home. She was currently finishing up her math class. I usually got out ten minutes before her. Sometimes because Mr. Jerr went long, often though it was because she got held up; either with friends or math problems she needed help with. I assumed that was what held her up today.

The sound of footsteps echoed against the emptying patio. Expecting Bethany, I turned my head and smiled. As fast as the smile appeared, it disappeared and my head snapped back away from the two bodies moving my way.

Lex and Cassy walked over, hand in hand. His head leaned closer to hers, his lips brushing against her ear as he whispered sweet nothings. A smile graced her face and pink tinted her cheeks.

I bit my lip in jealousy, trying not to picture what it would be like if I was the girl in his arms. How would it feel to hold his hand, and feel his lips again? What kind of things would he say to me? What would he say to elicit a blush, giggle, or smile?

The two of them stopped a few feet from me, still hand in hand. Cassy moved closer to him, her chest touching his. She blinked up at him, eyes wide and innocent. I almost snorted at the thought of Cassy being innocent. She was anything but.

"You want to come over later?" She tugged on his shirt gently as his arms slid around her waist.

"I can't tonight," he replied. "I've got plans."

Her bottom lip jutted out, eyebrows crinkling. "Fine. I'll see you later," she sighed.

I cringed and felt bile in my throat at the scene that unfolded in front of me. The sun peeked from behind the clouds, and the wind rustled Cassy's hair, her skirt billowing around her slim figure. Lex's shirt molded against his muscles and his blond hair gleamed gold. It was like the universe was intentionally creating beautiful scenery to make the romance even more intense.

Almost in slow motion, I saw as they leaned closer until their lips met. My stomach dropped and I turned away to avoid seeing anything else. In my chest, my heart ached for the boy I would never call my own.

"See ya," Cassy murmured with a low voice, before skipping off to the car that awaited her. When the gleaming silver car left the parking space I kept my eyes pointed at the ground.

Lex sighed, his hands slipping into his jeans pockets. He seemed oblivious to the fact I was there. Maybe if I was lucky, he wouldn't realize I was there and walk away without shooting an arrow into my heart with cruel words.

He turned around. "Hello, Honeybee." My nerves jumped at the easy tone to his voice. He was never casual with me, always curt and annoyed. *What is going on*? "Honeybee," he said again.

"What?" I tried to stay calm, but Lex had a way of making me severely nervous. Whether it was from the butterflies or fear of what he would say, I couldn't tell. At the moment it was probably a mix between the two. "What do you want?"

He grinned, his white teeth contrasting against his tan face. "You're still upset about this morning aren't you?"

Duh.

"Of course not," I muttered sarcastically. "Who wouldn't be overjoyed that their childhood stories were the butt of everyone's jokes?"

"I guess not you," he replied easily, his body moving to the spot next to me. My breath caught in my throat when his arm rested behind me. "Would you believe me if I said I was sorry?"

"No," I muttered. "You don't feel guilt."

He smirked, but said nothing.

Silence dragged on between the two of us, and I couldn't help but wonder why he was sitting next to me. Where was Bethany? She would know how to handle him. Of course, that would probably involve some sort of torture device and poisonous reptiles.

He cleared his throat, nabbing my attention from the line of ants moving toward poorly discarded lunch. "My mom wanted me to make sure you knew you were invited over to the house tonight, you and your mom."

I almost felt bad for him. His mom had no doubt forced him to ask me. Our parents weren't oblivious to the fact we had grown apart. I was pretty sure they were concocting a plan to get us to be friends again. I wouldn't mind a bit if they were. As much as I hated to admit it, I missed Lex and being able to trust him with things.

"I'll talk to her when I get home. I don't know if we're busy," I replied honestly.

A laugh escaped his lips. "I'm ninety percent sure your mom already knows and is planning to come, which is why I don't know my mom made me talk to you about it," he trailed off. "Anyways, knowing you, the only plan you might have is with that friend of yours." I glared at him. Just because that was true, didn't give him the right to make fun of my social life, or lack thereof. "Regardless of any plans you might have with Bridges, I don't think either one of us really have a choice. Knowing our moms, if we are anywhere but my backyard eating hotdogs tonight, we will be in big trouble."

"My mom loves me, maybe she won't subject me to spending more time with you," I mumbled under my breath.

A glint caught his eyes and he raised an eyebrow. "And what is wrong with spending time with me?" he questioned. "I am a joy to be around."

I scoffed. "To who? Those popular people you call your friends?" I grumbled, grabbing my backpack and standing up.

He caught my wrist. "Hang on, Honeybee,"

"What?" I snapped. "It's true."

"They're my friends," he argued. I rolled my eyes. They weren't his friends. There was no such thing as "friends" when it came to the popular group. "You just don't understand friendship because you only have one."

I resisted the urge to slap him. He was one of the reasons so few people spoke to me. Everything he told them made me an even bigger joke. They couldn't take me seriously, or see my face without remembering one of the many things they'd heard about me. "You're such a jerk." I bit my lip.

"And you're oversensitive." He stood up, walking past me. "See you tonight."

In the calmest possible mindset I could muster, I nodded and walked in the opposite direction. He would see me tonight. Hopefully the constant torment I put myself through wouldn't lead to my going insane.

When I found Bethany, she was pacing in front of one of the other buildings on campus. As soon as she saw me, she slapped her forehead. "Olivia, I'm so sorry." She walked over toward me.

"It's fine," I promised. "What happened?"

She sighed, running a hand through her hair. "I just got held up. First, I had to help my partner figure out the math problem before we could turn in our work. Then Jeremiah said he had something to give me and told me to wait here," she explained.

Jeremiah was on the football team, and had lately been trying to win the attention of my very own Bethany Bridges. She was so far out of his league, but he was popular so everyone thought it was weird he gave her any attention.

"I'm starting to think that maybe he isn't really going to get something from his locker, but is just biding his time to see how long an idiot like me will stay and wait for something that's not going to happen." She frowned.

"If he did, it's his loss," I told her, pushing my glasses farther up on my nose.

"Let's go." She looped her arm through mine and we walked back toward where she'd parked her car. The car had sat in the sun for the past seven hours and felt like a sauna when we got in. It was stifling and hard to breathe.

As soon as the car was turned on, we rolled our windows down. "So how was your day?" Her pointed brown eyes moved in my direction.

"Lex talked to me after my last class," I revealed.

"Do tell," she encouraged, laying her arm edge of her window. The sun soaked into her already tan skin, one of the pluses of living in California.

"It wasn't really a big deal. We argued a little, and he invited me over to his family barbecue tonight." I laughed when she slapped the steering wheel, her jaw lowered. "No biggie."

"Yeah right! That is the epitome of a *biggie*," she retorted. "Are you going?"

"Duh," I scoffed. "Even if my mom wasn't making me go, which she probably is, I would still go."

"Can I come?" Her eyes had a mischievous gleam to them. "You know I'm a joy at parties. And your mom loves me!"

I raised an eyebrow, and a smirk flitted across my lips. "She does, but last time you came to one of these parties you threw a cup of punch in Lex's face."

"I was only defending your honor. Excuse me for caring." She gasped.

"Well, you know what I mean. I don't want you to get in trouble on my behalf," I laughed.

"Tsk, tsk. Minor details," she replied. She stopped the car at the intersection, waiting for me to gather my things. My house was at the end of the street, not very far away. I snatched my bag off the bottom of the car and got out of the car. I shut the door and leaned in the window.

"I'll see you at my house in a half an hour, Livie. Don't you dare forget your bathing suit or there will be a very angry Bethany for you to deal with." she smiled sweetly.

"I would never." I winked. "See you then." With a wave, I headed down the road to get my things.

Chapter Two – Word Games

Ten minutes later, I was walking toward her house, a tank top covering my navy bikini top and leopard print boy shorts. My towel was draped over my shoulders. It was nearly four o'clock and the sun was still shining brightly in the sky. I pulled my long blonde hair up into a pony tail, feeling it bounce from side to side as I walked.

The sound of a car engine reached my ears, but I didn't think much of it. When the car honked, I jumped. My hands flew to my chest, as if to contain my heart from beating its way out of my chest. As I turned, the beat of my heart only intensified.

The cherry red shine of the jeep was almost blinding in the sun. Lex sat in the front seat, sunglasses over his eyes and a smile on his face. "Honeybee!"

"What do you want, Lex?" I muttered, turning to continue toward Bethany's.

"Where are you going?" He continued to drive by my side, his car moved slowly to match my pace. "Swimming?" He eyed the towel.

I held in my growl and nodded. "Yeah, what's it to you?" There was a stop sign not too far from where I was. Perhaps I could start sprinting when I got there and reach Bethany's house before he could torture me anymore. Not that his talking to me was really that torturous, but it wasn't helping my heart calm down.

"Do you want a lift?" Lex gestured to the passenger seat. I eyed it with disdain. "It's not going to kill you." He laughed. That's what he thought, but how could he even know that?

"No thanks." I kept walking. "I don't want to damage your reputation."

He laughed, shaking his head. "No one's around to see us anyways. Get in, Honeybee." Now I didn't even have a choice?

"I don't want a lift," I said again.

"It's not going to turn into a transformer and eat you, if that's what you're worried about."

"Goodbye, Lex." I turned down Bethany's street and was happy when the silence captured me again. But then it hit me. Lex never listened to me. I pushed away the fear that something was seriously wrong with him and kept walking.

When I got to Bethany's house, her mom let me in.

"Hi, Olivia," Karen Bridges greeted. Her rusty brown hair and blue eyes were a stark difference from Bethany's looks. Of course that made sense considering Bethany was from China, and adopted by the Bridges when Bethany was two years old.

"Hi," I replied.

"Bethany's in the back," she told me, closing the door after me. I nodded my thanks and moved through their house toward the patio door that led to the pool. Their house was large, with white couches in the living room and a hardwood floor in the kitchen. Glossy countertops gleamed in the sunlight that streamed through the window.

I pushed open the glass door and closed it gently behind me so Bethany wouldn't realize I was there. She had her back to me, sitting on the edge of the pool with her feet in the water. I snuck toward her, holding in my laughter.

Just as I was about to grab her shoulders and push her in, her head swiveled toward me, eyebrow raised accusingly. "You can't sneak up on someone in flip flops." I frowned. "What took you so long? I was about to call the cops," she joked.

"I couldn't find my towel, and then Lex stopped me on the side of the road," I informed her. I shaded my eyes against the glare off the pool. *Where did I put my sunglasses?* They were in my bag somewhere.

She wrinkled her nose. "Did he offer you candy if you got in the car?"

I chortled. "That would make more sense than him actually being nice to me." I let my towel and swimming bag drop to the ground beside me. "Something is seriously wrong with that boy."

"Maybe he's dying, and has to right his wrongs before he goes!" She said cheerily.

My expression dropped and I held in the eye roll. *Only Bethany.* With a swift shove, I sent her into the pool.

A few seconds later, her head shot up, and she coughed. "You jerk," she hissed, rubbing the water from her eyes.
"You were happy about Lex dying, you kind of deserved it." She swam back toward the edge of the pool. I moved away so she couldn't reach me.

"To think! A boy is coming between us!" She exclaimed pulling herself out of the pool. She shook water at me.

"You hate him, and I love him. It automatically makes him come between us."

"Yeah, yeah, whatever," she mumbled, wringing her hair out. "I'm just annoyed that he is the boy that is coming between us."

"If it wasn't him, it would be someone else." I said, glancing at the pool. The Bridge's backyard was fenced all around, with afew lawn chairs were around the pool, a towel draped over one of them. I'd always wanted a pool, but having a best friend with a pool was a good substitute.

"I thought we were going to go swimming."

"I did," she said dryly. I grinned. "But by all means, go get your swim on." She waved her hand toward the pool.

The water seemed to be calling out to me, and the heat only made it more inviting.

"I might have, too," I murmured. I stood up and shed the tank top, laying it on the chair.

"You know, dressed like that I can kind of understand why Lex would offer you a ride," she noted. I raised an eyebrow. "You're gorgeous, Olivia. Most boys would want to offer you a ride."

"Yet they never do," I pointed out, sitting on the edge of the pool.

"Considering the things I've heard from some of the guys, Lex makes it like you're off limits. My friend Ron thought you were cute, but Lex talked to him and convinced him to leave you alone," she told me.

I turned around and looked at her, my legs dangling the water. "Really?"

She nodded and stood up. She struggled out of her wet green t-shirt, the wet material clinging to her body. "Yeah."

"That doesn't make any sense," I mumbled, leaving the safety of the ledge and slipping into the water. I shivered slightly, letting my body adjust to the water temperature.

"It's Lex. Since when does anything he does make sense?" she laughed, jumping into the pool. I turned away, avoiding being splashed in the face. When she resurfaced, she floated on her back. "But honestly, what do you think is going on?"

I shrugged, treading water. "Maybe he really is sick." I bit back a frown. "What if he really is trying to right his wrongs?" I wondered.

"I don't know," she murmured.

Me either.

Taking a deep breath, I slipped under the water. It comforted me in a gentle caress. The chlorine stung my eyes when I opened them, swimming toward the shallower end of the pool. My lungs were burning by the time I got to the other end and burst through the surface, gulping in the air. Water trickled down my face, I insistently wiped it away.

"Olivia," Bethany mumbled. I glanced at her, wiping away water before it could fall into my eyes. She was still lying on her back, eyes closed.

"Yes?"

"Do you think Lex likes you?" At her words I burst out laughing at the absurdity. She turned over in the water to glare at me. "I'm serious," she claimed.

"Beth, there is no possible way in this world that Lex has any romantic feelings for me," I told her, laughing still. "This is Lex we're talking about. The guy who took my first kiss and walked away, the same guy who embarrasses me for fun, and tells other guys to stay away. If this is his way of showing he likes me, he is seriously messed up in the head."

"Boys always get messed up in the head when it comes to girls," she assured me, still seemingly convinced that Lex liked me. As much as I liked the idea, it made my heart beat faster, I couldn't think that way. Lex didn't like me. If I let myself believe otherwise, I would only end up with further heartbreak. He had caused me too much pain already. I wasn't going to let him hurt me anymore if I could help it.

"Jeremiah seems to have the right idea. He was bringing you presents!" I threw my arms up dramatically, water splashing. "I'm a terrible friend for not letting you stay."

She chuckled, rolling her eyes. "Yeah, you are. What do you think he was bringing me?"

I shrugged carelessly, swimming toward the edge. "Just an engagement ring and some famous singer to assist him in the proposal." I pulled myself from the water and laid down to work on my tan.

Bethany laughed and got out as well. "Of course. What else could he possibly have for me?" I smiled and let my eyes close, fishing my sunglasses out before relaxing into the sunshine.

"Call me after the party is over," Bethany said, waving as I walked out the front door.
"I will!" I waved the tank top at her, droplets flying from the ends and slapping her in the face. She glared, but I could see the smile dying to break free. It was her fault for throwing me in the pool before I was planning to leave. All because I stole a few chips when she wasn't looking. The punishment didn't seem to fit the crime at all.

Walking home, I felt kind of exposed in my bikini top and boy shorts out there for anyone passing by to see. My mother wouldn't have approved, but hopefully she wouldn't have to know. My wet hair was in a messy pony tail, dripping down my back occasionally. Sunglasses shaded my eyes, though the sun was starting to set so it wasn't as bright. It was nearing six o'clock, and a text from

Mom told me the barbeque started in an hour. I wasn't looking forward to it.

I was nearing the neighborhood when I saw the devil himself. Well, *almost*. Lex and a few of his friends were walking toward me. I prayed that they wouldn't recognize me. Maybe they would be too preoccupied with each other to notice me.

One of his friends was the first to notice me. His eyes traveled up my body, and a grin appeared on his lips. I almost wanted to scoff. Of course, the first guy to really take an interest in my looks was one of Lex's low-life friends.

The creeper hit Lex and the other guy, who both looked up to see me. I willed my cheeks too stay a neutral color. I wanted to gasp when Lex seemed to be checking me out as well. There had to be something wrong with his brain.

"Hey baby, where have you been all of my life?" the first guy asked. I rolled my eyes. They weren't even creative. How pathetic.

"Hiding, obviously," I muttered. Lex raised an eyebrow in my direction, his eyes seemingly raking over my body even closer. I resisted the urge to shudder, and moved on.

"See you tonight, honey," Lex quipped as I passed. I stopped dead in my tracks, his friends snickering. *He knew it was me*? And he didn't say something?

A strange sensation filled me and made me turn around. "Can't wait," I cooed. The two guys smirked, glancing to see what Lex would do.

He simply grinned. "I'll be sure to set an extra place at dinner."

"What time should I come over?" I smiled back.

He raised an eyebrow, like he hadn't expected me to continue the charade. "Seven?"

"Is there a dress code?"

He eyed my body again, sending a shiver down my spine. "What you've got on now is perfectly fine," he answered. I didn't know how to respond to that. "I'll see you tonight," he winked, clearly thinking he had won. "Maybe I'll show you my bedroom," his lowered his voice seductively.

My breath hitched. Did he really just say that? Had he forgotten he had a girlfriend? My heart was racing, and my mind was spinning, trying to think of a comeback.

"Cat got your tongue?" he chuckled.

Pinching myself mentally, I shook my head. "No. I'm just surprised. What makes you think I would want to see your room?" I turned my head, noticeably checking him out. "Okay looks, below average intelligence…" I shrugged. "I think I'll pass," I sneered. With that, I turned on my heel and walked away before he could say anything else.

"You're losing your touch, bro," one of the guys laughed

A smile flitted across my features. I had never beat Lex at one of his games before. First time for everything.

Chapter Three – Barbeque

When I walked in the house I could smell baked beans. No doubt Mom was making food for the barbeque tonight. I dropped my stuff by the door. I would deal with it soon enough.

I glanced around. Wood flooring ran throughout the entire house except the upstairs, where tan carpet covered the floors. Pictures of family and friends adorned the sky blue walls. Dark tan couches occupied the living room, and a matching wood table and chairs were in the dining room, covered with business papers and bills. Mom worked at a law firm as an assistant.

"Mom," I called out, heading toward the kitchen. She was leaning over a pan on the stove top. She had changed from her work clothes to a pair of shorts and a white blouse. She turned as I came in. She scowled, noting that I wasn't wearing anything to cover my stomach.

"Bethany pushed me into the pool today." It was better to play the defensive part before she could get mad at me for wearing so little in public.

She frowned, shaking her head. "Sure she did." She always sided with Bethany. I didn't understand why she was more trustworthy than I was. "I would chew you out, but I'm in a hurry. I'm helping Patty and Steve set up."

Nodding, I plucked a grape from the fruit bowl and popped it in my mouth. "The Diamond's and their parties," I murmured. "What time does it start?"

"Seven," she answered. "And you had better be there on time."

"I will," I promised, giving her a hug. "I'm taking a shower. I'll come over when I'm done." She waved and I walked out of the kitchen and upstairs to get some clothes to wear.

My bedroom was the second door on the left. Mom's was on the right, and the upstairs bathroom was next to my room. I pushed open the door and looked at my room in disdain. It was a tragedy I wasn't the neat freak that Mom was. My room was left in utter chaos most of the time, including today. Clothes were strewn about; homework pages littered my desk along with graded assignments and dishes.

My full size bed was unmade, the black comforter haphazardly thrown on, big pillows pushed against the headrest. The nightstand near my bed had a half full glass of water and a bright green lamp.

"I really should clean this up," I mumbled, stepping around the pile of clothes to get to my dresser.

"Livie, you can't leave this stuff in the entry way!" Mom yelled from downstairs. I would've replied, but the door slammed so I knew she had already left for across the street.

Shrugging, I pulled open my drawers in search of something to wear. Knowing the Diamond's, it was a causal party and I didn't have to worry about dressing up or trying to impress anyone.

Humming, I grabbed a pair of black leggings and a sweetheart neckline dress, with a green and blue floral pattern. A strapless bra and underwear came next, and then I headed down the hall to take a shower and rid myself of the chlorine smell. I didn't hate smelling like a pool, but my skin felt so dried out after swimming that a shower and lotion were usually mandatory afterwards.

I stripped out of my bathing suit and showered quickly. When I was out, I smelled like a mix of raspberry and vanilla instead of chlorine. I felt refreshed and soft again, instead of tired and restricted.

"Why must my hair hate me so?" I pulled a brush through my hair, cringing at the tangles it caught on. As I worked on brushing it out, I tried to figure out how I was going to style it. Bethany was always better at this kind of thing, so I decided to call her.

"This had better be important. Edward just asked Bella to marry him," she muttered, a hint of humor to her voice. That was almost always how she answered my phone calls.

I laughed, shaking my head. "Sorry."

She sighed in mock frustration. "You always interrupt me when I'm getting to the good parts," she muttered.

"I know. I'm terrible."

"You are," she agreed. "What's up?"

"How should I do my hair?"

It was her turn to laugh this time. "Really?" I nodded, even though she couldn't see me. "Do it cute. You have to impress that stupid boyfriend of yours," she mumbled.

"He's not my boyfriend," I told her.

"You wish he was," she shot back. "And I have no idea. A cute pony tail, or a head band, maybe a fancy braid. I spent too much time in the sun today so I'm kind of out of it."

"Bethany, you're failing me." She snorted. "That's not an attractive sound," I informed her, looking at my limp hair in the mirror.

"That's not a very nice thing to say to someone," she sighed. "And I don't know how to help you. Just dry it, and put a few little braids in it. I'm sure you'll look great no matter what." Her suggestion wasn't bad, so I would probably end up doing that. "Oh, and wear natural looking makeup, nothing to bold. I read an article online that said guys are into natural beauties."

I chortled. "Don't believe everything you read on internet. But I'll take it into consideration."

"Sounds good. Anything else?" she asked, yawning through her words.

"Nope. Get back to your nap," I replied. "I'll call you later."

"Okay. Bye." She hung up the phone.

My dress lay on the bed. It occurred to me that I was walking around my room in a bra and leggings, and that my window curtain wasn't closed, so I hurried to put on the dress. Once I was dressed, I blow dried my hair and twisted some braids into it. I almost looked like a hippie. I applied some mascara and a little blush, defining my cheeks. Feeling almost prepared to go see Lex, I left my room and headed downstairs.

My bag and wet clothes were still on the floor. Sighing, I picked them up, careful not to drip on the carpet too much and deposited them in the laundry room. I'd do laundry when I got home later. Slipping some sandals on, I headed outside and across the street.

Mom was in the backyard, sitting at a table with Mr. and Mrs. Diamond, or Steve and Patty. Steve looked like an older version of Lex, except his hair was darker and he didn't have an eighteen year old body anymore. Patty's brown hair and eyes were still youthful, a bright smile always lit up her face. Lex definitely got his good looks from his parents.

"Livie," Mom said, waving me over. I smiled and walked over, hugging the Diamond's.

"Hey sweetheart," Patty cooed, patting my back. "How are you?" The hints of a southern twang lingered in her voice. She lived in Victoria, Texas for a while before she moved to California and met Steve.

"I'm good, how are you?" I replied.

"Wonderful." She beamed. "You should go get something to eat. Lex said some of his soccer teammates were going to come over later." I nodded my thanks and moved toward the food table.

As I picked out my food, I glanced around, searching for the familiar blond locks. The Diamond's back yard was a lovely dark green, with patches of colorful flowers placed around. A fountain of a turtle sat near the back of their yard.

"Looking for someone?" a voice whispered in my ear. His body was so close behind me I could feel his shirt brush against my back.

"Trying to avoid them is more like it." I grabbed my plate of food and headed back to the table.

Lex grasped my wrist, pulling my body closer to his. "It's kind of hard to avoid someone when you're at their house, don't you think?" Ignoring him, I pulled away and walked to the table. Slipping into the seat next to Mom, I smiled politely and listened to the conversations around me.

Soon after, Lex slid into the spot across from me, shooting his parents and Mom a smile. I resisted the urge to roll my eyes when he didn't even acknowledge me. I focused on my food. When nothing and no one else wanted to be my friend, food was something I could rely on. I frowned. I sounded so pathetic in my head.

I glanced down just in time to see Lex sneak his hand across the table and steal a few chips. My jaw dropped. "Really?"

"I live here. Technically, all this food belongs to me," he justified his actions. I rolled my eyes and looked away, sliding my arm in front of my plate so he wouldn't have such an open range.

I continued eating, shooting glares at Lex occasionally. He smiled, but otherwise ignored me. It stung how easy I was to ignore. Grumbling to myself, I stabbed my fork against the plastic plate.

"Livie." I looked up at Patty. "Did you hear me?" I raised an eyebrow questioningly. *She had asked me something*? I needed to spend more time in the real world and less time among my thoughts.

"Obviously not," Lex chided.

"Sorry, what did you say?" I wondered.

"I was asking if you were done," she said, glancing down at my plate. A frown took my face captive when I looked down to see it was empty. The hot dog and fruit I had finished, but I'd still had a few more chips to eat. They of course, magically appeared in Lex's hands.

"I suppose I am." I sent a glare at Lex before looking back at his mom. "Why?"

"Well, it's just, we don't really have a lot planned for tonight, mainly a lot of adults talking, and eating. You and Lex are the only young people here. The rest of the boys won't be here for a while. Perhaps you two would want to go see a movie, or something like that instead of hanging out with a bunch of old timers," she drawled.

The idea sent my nerves into frenzy. "No, that's fine."

"I knew you hated me," Lex murmured, almost genuinely sad.

"You're such a drama queen," I muttered.

"At least I'm royalty, you're just a lowly peasant," he retorted. A wind brushed by, ruffling his hair.

I set my chin in the palm of my hand, giving him a sweet smile. "And you wonder why I hate you."

"Touché," he winked, grabbing a soda from the table and taking a drink. When he finished, he stood up from the table. "Alright, we're leaving."

"We?" Patty asked. He nodded, and came around to my side of the table. I nearly fell when he jerked the chair out from under me. "Lex!" she scolded.

He'd saved me from the ground, catching me a little too high around my waist. "She's fine." He let me go after I pushed his arms away. I nearly stumbled again, but managed to catch myself before I fell.

"Define that word why don't you," I muttered, glaring up at him. He shot me a grin.

"Where are you guys going to go?" Mom asked, ever the worry wart. But since I was leaving with Lex, the odds of my demise being in the next few hours become considerably higher.

"Wherever the wind takes us," he breathed wistfully.

"Lex," Steve bit out. There was an undertone of anger to his voice. I'd heard it often when Steve and Lex talked to each other.

He sighed, shaking his head at his parents. "Probably across the street." He grabbed my arm and started walking away. I had no choice but to follow helplessly after him.

"Keep my daughter out of trouble." Mom laughed.

I nearly scoffed at her words. Did she not know the boy she was letting me walk away with? Lex was the very definition of trouble. I seriously needed to have a conversation with her about parenting.

Chapter Four – Kidnapped by Crush, Send Help

When we had cleared the backyard, and prying eyes, Lex dropped my arm. I didn't know where we were going, but anywhere with Lex was doomed to be dangerous. I hated that I was so excited to be walking next to him. Stupid female emotions.

His hands slipped into his pockets. "I must say, this afternoon I was impressed." He glanced sideways. "Well done, Honeybee."

I wanted to glare at the blush that crept to my cheeks. "I guess after spending enough time with Bethany her snarky attitude rubbed off on me."

He chuckled, his head lolling back. "I wasn't talking about what you said." He kicked a rock, sending it flying across the road toward my mailbox.

"What?"

He let a low whistle escape his lips, his dark eyes darting toward me. "You have become kind of hot since the last time I saw you in your skivvies."

"Did you seriously use the word skivvies?" I deadpanned. It wasn't logical to talk about that first rather than the fact he had been totally inappropriate, but the word *skivvies* wasn't something someone used every day.

"I did." He nodded.

"Don't talk about me that way." I kept walking toward the house, heading for the front door.

"Where do you think you're going?" Lex questioned, taking hold of my arm again and bringing me toward the backyard.

"Where do you think *you're* going?" I snapped, knowing exactly where he was going. Maybe I would be wrong, and he just wanted to chill in the backyard.

"The tree house."

My hopes plummeted. The last time we had been in the tree house together, he'd kissed me and then walked away. One of my greatest heartaches took place in the tree house, and he expected me to go up there with him willingly?

"Honeybee, come on."

I grimaced. "I don't want to, Lex. I haven't been up there in for a long time." *Lie.* "There are probably bugs up there." *Lie.* "Maybe even a nest of squirrels." *Lie.* I was up there pretty often. Homework or late night slumber parties often led to spending time in the tree house. Any bugs were killed and the tree house was sprayed, especially when it was related to spiders.

"How bad can it be?" he shrugged, resting his hand on one of the rungs of the ladder.

"Pretty bad," I said, biting my lip and wrinkling my eyebrows in an attempt to convince him I was actually worried about going up there.

"I'll protect you," he crooned. "Now get your butt up there." He slapped the ladder and dropped my arm.

Glaring, I crossed my arms. "So you can look up my dress? I don't think so, perv. You go first. After all, how can you protect me from behind me?"

"I'm amazing," he offered, a sly grin on his lips.

"If we're going to go up in the tree house, you're going first." He sighed, dropping his eyes. I smiled triumphantly.

"Fine." He started up the ladder, looking back at me. "But if you wanted to stare at my butt so much, you could've just said so." I wasn't even going to dignify that with a response.

When he was far enough up, I went up behind him. As I reached the top, I saw him looking around the tree house. He had to slouch slightly, having grown since the last time he was here.

The small wood house had one window looking out over the street below. The door had a few strings of beads still; most of them had fallen apart over the years. There was a small table near the back wall, two purple bags, and a small bookshelf lined with classic fairy tales. In reality, it was my escape.

"Yeah, this place is crawling with bugs," he agreed sarcastically. I crossed my arms and looked away. He moved over to the window, leaning down. "Still there."

I knew he meant our initials. When we were twelve, he'd gotten out his pocketknife and carved our initials into the wood so anyone who saw them would know we would stay best friends forever. It killed me inside to know that we weren't best friends, we weren't even friends. We were strangers who knew too much about each other.

"Where else would they be?"

"I thought maybe they liked traveling," he replied, stepping away from the carving. There was some kind of emotion in his eyes, almost like he remembered the promise we'd made that day six years ago.

"No, they're good where they're at." I moved to the window, leaning against the side of it. He glanced at me, biting his lip before looking away. My body went into overdrive when he leaned next to me. I couldn't take it anymore. Something was going on with him, and I needed to find out. "Lex, are you dying?" The words fell from my mouth before I could even comprehend saying them.

Way to be tactful, Olivia.

Lex's eyebrows were raised, and his jaw was slightly open. He stared at me in silence for a few moments before he responded. "What?" I looked away. "Why would you ask me something like that?"

"I don't know. Let's talk about something else," I suggested, hoping he would drop it.

He didn't. "No, come on. That's not something people ask me every day. Do you know something I don't?" he laughed, nudging my shoulder with his. If only he knew how much that little brush did to my mind.

"What? No, of course not," I mumbled, averting my gaze. My mind started to play scenarios where the two of us hugged, and he whispered into my ear, bringing a blush to my cheeks.

"Honeybee," he whined. "Just tell me." When I didn't reply he poked me in the side, making me jerk away from him. "If you don't tell me, there will be more where that comes from." Now he was threatening me? How mature.

"Okay, fine," I relented. "You've been acting weird. I thought maybe you were trying to right your wrongs or something."

"Did you and Bridges concoct this explanation?" he wondered, a crooked grin giving him a boyish innocence.

"Maybe."

He leaned closer to me, inches away from my face. I swear his eyes flickered to my lips. My breath hitched when he poked my nose. "That's really stupid." He looked around the tree house again. "It's been a long time since I've been up here with you," he mentioned.

I let out the breath I'd held in when his words connected. I quirked an eyebrow. "Does that mean you've been up here *without* me?"

"I think it's more fun if you don't know the answer to that," he winked.

I gaped, slapping his arm. "You're such a creeper! Bethany was right!"

"What?" He laughed, not bothering to turn and look at me.

"Bethany had her suspicions, but this proves it. You're stalking me. Admit it," I challenged.

He turned his head toward me. "You caught me, I'm stalking you. I watch you sleep, eat, and shower."

I slapped him. "You're a pig." Hopefully the glare I had going was intimidating or at least a tad angry looking. He couldn't make comments like that and expect that I wouldn't be offended. I wasn't a feminist, but I wasn't grateful for those kinds of comments.

"I thought I was a drama queen?" he prodded.

Biting my lip, I just shook my head refusing to talk. Lex Diamond could leave, but I wasn't going to talk to him until he apologized for his comments. Silence stretched between us. I felt proud of the two minute silence. That was a long time for me to ignore Lex.

He sighed. "Seems like this friendship never works, huh?" he was baiting me, trying to get me to talk to him. He never wanted to talk, but all of a sudden sitting in silence with me wasn't acceptable? "Our moms have been pushing us to be friendly with each other for a while."

"Waste of time." *Weakling.* I couldn't even last five minutes.

His eyes lit up when I spoke. How was it possible to be so dark, yet so endearing? "Right? But they can't be stopped. I think they must've had some sort of bet, or maybe a deal. When we moved in and started hanging out as kids, I bet you fifty bucks our moms planned out that you and I would get married." I felt my heart drop into my stomach. Knowing our moms, he was probably right. His careless attitude only proved that he had no feelings romantically for me whatsoever. Bethany was way off.

"I bet you fifty-two bucks they picked out the venue and first dance song," I added, feeling a shake in my voice.

"I guess it makes sense though," he shrugged. "Them wanting their kids to get married one day. I mean, it's like the plot line to every stupid romance movie."

My feelings fit a stupid romance movie, great. "Totally." I bit my lip, willing all my emotions to stay in check.

"They're probably pushing this fake friendship thing because they're still holding onto the hope that one day their children will magically fall in love and become that cute couple from the movie."

"You're probably right," I agreed halfheartedly. I wanted us to be that cute couple so bad it hurt.

"Did you tell your mom about that awkward kiss?"

He was joking about my first kiss. *Our* first kiss. I found it to be so magical and perfect, but of course he found it awkward.

"Maybe." What fourteen-year old girl didn't gush about that to their mom? "Did you tell your buddies you got to second base?" I muttered sarcastically.

He smirked, bumping my shoulder. "No. I barely knew what that meant when I was fourteen." He glanced over at me. "I bet your mom told my mom. So technically it's your fault that this is still going on. That kiss probably kept their hope alive."

I turned to him, my eyes hard. "If I recall correctly, you initiated that kiss. Not me. The fact it got back to your mother isn't my fault. You didn't *have* to kiss me. There were plenty of other girls who would've kissed you."

"Yeah, but why would I want to kiss a girl I didn't know?" he asked.

"Maybe so you wouldn't have to deal with your mothers trying to put you together down the road," I muttered, standing.

"I'm a boy. I don't think that far into the future," he told me. I smirked. That much was true. He sighed, turning to look at me.

"What?"

"You know, they probably think we're really into each other," he admitted.

"Do you have a point coming up any time soon or can I leave?" I asked, feeling the rapid beat of my heart. *I hope he can't hear it.*

He grinned. "I do have a point. I'm just not sure what it is."

Taking a deep breath, I smiled. "Are you trying to tell me that you're actually in love with me? Because that's what I'm hearing. You seem to be pointing out how our moms were right."

He shrugged. "Maybe they were. I mean, obviously I'm a sexy beast so you're bound to be attracted to me."

I bit the inside of my cheek to stop any emotion from spreading across my features. "You've got that going for you."

"And I'm stalking you, so I must be attracted to you on some level," he murmured, his eyes flickering away.

My breath seemed to stop short when my brain caught up with how close Lex and I were. *When did he lean closer?* Or did I do that? "I'd like to think I'm not hideous."

He grinned, brushing hair away from my eyes. "You're not."

"Complimenting me huh?" I questioned, watching his tongue run across his lips. "You totally like me."

"Is that excitement I hear in your voice?" he noted.

"No. You like me remember?" My heart beat faster. "Not the other way around," I replied.

"Of course, I forgot." His hand slid to the back of my neck. "Well, we both know how impulsive I am. If I'm the one who likes you, you better expect the unexpected."

"But by expecting the unexpected it defeats the purpose," I pointed out.

He shook his head. "Just shut up-"

A burst of bravery shot through my veins. "I believe the next part of that sentence is 'and kiss me'."

He grinned. "Don't have to ask me twice."

My eyes closed on their own accord as his lips captured mine. He angled his head, deepening the kiss. Our lips melded together; touching and exploring. His other hand moved to my waist, pulling our bodies closer together. I gasped softly when his lips left mine, traveling down my neck, brushing across my shoulder. He moved my body away from the window, pushing me against the wall. His body pressed against mine, his warmth enveloping my senses. I couldn't believe this was happening again. Butterflies flitted into my stomach, dancing around my insides. His lips moved back to mine.

Time seemed to slow down when we finally pulled away to breathe. His eyes were alive, and his face flushed. I imagined I looked similar to him. He leaned his head against mine, stroking my face gently. I leaned into his touch.

He looked like he was about to kiss me again when his phone started going off. He jolted, pulling back. The warmth he offered left, and I held in my shiver. Lex pulled his phone out and cringed.

"What's wrong?" my voice was soft.

"I have to go." He started toward the ladder.

"What?" *Déjà vu.* "You can't be serious."

"I'm sorry." My hopes lifted somewhat. "This was a mistake." *And there went the hope.* He started to climb down the ladder without saying anything else.

"You're a jerk, and I'm an idiot," I muttered under my breath, blinking back tears. "Everything we've done together has been a mistake." I glanced out the window and saw him talking on the phone as he walked toward his house. He was smiling, speaking animatedly to whoever was on the other side of the phone. My gut instinct, and the look on his face, told me it was Cassy.

My eyes stung, but I refused to let my tears fall on his account. My heart was done breaking over him. *I hope.* When I got inside the house, I went to my room and called Bethany.

"Hey, what's up?" she answered cheerily.

I bit my lip, trying to focus my emotions elsewhere. "Can I come over?"

"What happened?" she asked knowingly.

"I'll tell you when I get there," I murmured, pressing my palms against my eyes.

"Okay. See you soon," she said softly before hanging up.

I quickly packed a backpack, throwing in the needed clothes and toiletries, and then I headed out. I left a note for Mom so she would know I hadn't been kidnapped or murdered.

When I got to Bethany's house, she was waiting at the door. A light blue dress danced around her, the wind playing with the material. Her arms were crossed and she frowned. "Do I get to hear what happened now?"

Nodding, I followed her upstairs to her room where I told her everything that had happened. I felt so stupid afterwards. Only an idiot would let Lex mess with their heart, let alone hand it to him.

"That guy is getting on my last nerve!" she growled.

"H-how can I love him?" I pulled my hair from my face, twisting it into a bun.

"You can't help it," she told me.

"I have to get over him," I muttered, wiping at my eyes. Tears were lingering on the edge, almost ready to spill.

"You will." She hugged a pink pillow to her chest. Her brown bedspread was lumpy in the middle, proof of her quick attempt to clean up before I got there.

"How?" Even after all the crap he put me through, I still cared about him. I still wanted to be with him, for him to want me back. The love I felt for him wasn't going to disappear overnight.

"We're going to the mall tomorrow, and we're going boy shopping," she told me, nodding her head. She was determined.

"Boy shopping?" I coughed out a laugh. Somehow I didn't think going shopping for boy stuff was going to help at all.

She grinned from ear to ear. "We're going to find you a new boy."

Chapter Five – Boy Shopping

"How about that one?" Bethany asked, pointing to the boy who was holding bags for his mother.

"No, I don't think that's a good idea. He looks a little young." I laughed, taking in the boy's Mario Kart t-shirt.

"Oh come on, he's so cute!" She argued, looping her arm through mine.

"He's seven," I said, dragging her away. The mall was full of people, everyone out and about. I never understood how so many people had the money and time to go to the mall so often. It wasn't like the mall was ever empty, or barely crowded. There were always people inside the shops, and walking around with a billion bags.

"Fine, but he's still cute," she mumbled, sighing. "Oh, let's go in here. I need to get a new dress for my grandparent's anniversary." She moved into one of the numerous stores. Her light pink skirt sashayed around her legs. The white blouse was tucked in, and she wore a brown belt that matched her ankle boots. Her hair was in a high pony tail, bangs brushing her eyebrows. She looked like she'd just walked off a photo shoot.

I felt so frumpy in comparison. White cut off shorts, a purple tank with bright blue stripes, and a pair of leopard print flats. Some of my hair was clipped back, and my glasses were propped on my nose. I was not going to win any hearts dressed so casually. Bethany on the other hand…

"Hurry up," she called over her shoulder, already looking at different dresses. Sighing, I walked in the store and moved to stand next to her. "How about this one?" she pulled out a knee length dress, with ruffles around the V-neck. The dark ebony color would wash out her skin tone.

"No, you need something lighter."

She put the dress back on the hanger. "I know. Maybe I could borrow something. Do you still have that orange dress, with the yellow stitching?" she asked.

"I was going to give it to you as a birthday present, but if you need it now that's fine. I'm sure I'll be able to find something else," I said, sighing at the end. She loved that dress, and I never wore it. It seemed like the perfect present. Now I would have to find something else.

"What?!" she gasped, clasping her hands over her mouth. "Really?" she squeaked. I nodded and cringed when she squealed again. "You're the best friend ever. Seriously."

"I know." I shrugged carelessly. "Are we done shopping for a dress now?" I questioned.

"Yeah, let's go. Now I really need to find you a new boy." She pulled me out of the store and back into the crowd of people.

"Or you could buy me ice cream," I offered. "I think I'd like that more anyways."

She grinned, raising any eyebrow slightly. "How about frozen yogurt?"

I drew my eyebrows together. Something had to be wrong with the frozen yogurt. Why else would she look so mischievous about it? "Sure."

"Great!" Bethany cheered, moving easily through the crowd. She was so petite that she was able to move around without much trouble. Most other people, myself included, had to wait for a clear pathway before continuing.

Since she couldn't be bothered to wait for me, I lost Bethany in the hustle of the crowd. Thankfully, I knew the only frozen yogurt place was in the food court, and the food court wasn't far from where I was. When I got there, I was instantly hit with the smell of fried foods and overworked people. I wrinkled my nose in distaste and looked around for Bethany.

Plastic tables were arranged in lines in the center of the very large, open area. People were spread around the area, taking up nearly every inch of room. It was like my entire high school, and then some, were piling into the food court for lunch. Teens laughed and talked, a few elderly couples shared dinners, and the occasional security officer leered at the girls passing by them. I made a note to walk far around those guards.

I looked around again, searching for Bethany in this mass of bodies hoping she hadn't deserted me in the mall, of all places. "Where are you," I murmured, squinting as I looked around.

"You're so racist."

I jumped, turning to face Bethany who stood there, a new shopping bag dangling from her arm. "How am I racist?"

"So I'm Chinese. That doesn't mean you can stand there squinting at me for like five minutes. That's not exactly polite," she mumbled, a tone of sarcasm on the edge of her voice. "Whatever. Let's go. Frozen yogurt already has a line a mile long." I moved quicker this time so as not to lose her in the crowd. "I found some cute earrings." She shook the newest addition to her pile of bags.

"You left me to buy earrings?" I frowned. "I thought you loved me more than material possessions."

"They were on sale. I love you, but come on. Sometimes I just can't help it," she admitted, stopping as we reached the line. Families, teens, and kids stood in a huge line in front of us. We would never make it to the front, at least not before I gained gray hair and stronger glasses. "By the way, since we're here, there is a really cute guy who works up at the counter," she mentioned.

And her true reasoning comes out.

"I see." My eyes traveled past the horde of humans in front of me, looking for the boy she spoke of.

"He's got black hair, nice smile, and he's helping that woman with twelve kids," she told me, waving her hand in the direction of the front. My eyes caught onto the woman with *four* kids, and moved past her to the guy helping them.

He had hair as dark as the night sky, chocolate eyes shining back at one of the kids blabbering on to him about something. The uniform he wore was all white, with the logo of frozen yogurt on the pocket. The light pink stood out against the white. A paper hat, like one worn in old time candy shops, was pushed down on his head. The uniform formed to his body as he moved, reaching around one of his co-workers to get something. He smiled once more as he handed the little girl a plastic hot pink spoon. The mom thanked him and moved on with her kids in tow.

"You're staring," Bethany remarked, elbowing me.

"You pointed him out, I'm simply making sure he's worth noticing," I explained, grinning.

"And?" she prodded.

I shrugged. "He's not bad." *Lie.* He was definitely attractive. Tall, dark, and handsome fit him perfectly.

"Not bad? He's the best looking guy we've seen all day!" She grumbled as quietly as possible.

"What about the last guy?" I shrunk beneath her glare. "Okay, little boy. He was cute," I argued.

"Get real, Olivia," she sighed. "You better make me proud and flirt with this boy when we finally get to the front. Think about what you're going to say now."

"Bethany," I groaned. "He probably gets hit on all the time. There's literally a group of girls standing over there gawking at him." She turned and saw the group of pre-teen girls swooning as they watched him from a distance. "We were never like that, right?" I cringed.

"No, of course not," she dismissed the idea.

"Good."

"But you're still flirting with him, or so help me I will do something you won't like," she threatened. Out of spite, I decided not to flirt with him. Plus, if I tried to flirt, I would embarrass myself and go home feeling even worse. What was the worst Bethany could do? She wouldn't pull any stunts that resembled something Lex would do.

After a while, we finally came to the front of the line. He smiled brightly at us. "Hello, ladies. What can I get you?" Bethany jabbed me with her elbow, making me jump. The boy bit back a laugh.

"Olivia, you go first. Tell the boy what you want," she said, purposefully using my name.

I stared up at the menu. "I don't know," I trailed off, pursing my lips like I was thinking really hard about what I wanted.

"You were looking up at the counter for fifteen minutes. How do you still not know?" she questioned. I shrugged. She rolled her eyes. "You're going to hold the line up. And there are a lot of people who want to get their frozen yogurt."

"You could order you know," I informed her. She frowned at me. I returned the gesture by sticking my tongue out at her.

"I don't mean to rush you, but we do have a lot of people to get to," the boy said, the polite smile still lighting up his face. If only it was that easy for me to be attractive.

"Sorry," Bethany mumbled, glancing once more at me. She quickly gave him her order, and he gave the details to someone else who started putting it together for her.

He glanced at me, raising an eyebrow expectantly. "Do you know what you want?" Bethany gave me a pointed look before turning back to him.

Oh no.

"She wants your number."

I gasped, staring at her with wide eyes and a slack jaw. The frozen yogurt guy smirked, glancing at me. I didn't dare look back at him. My cheeks were flaming bright red. My own best friend betrayed me.

She smiled sweetly at me. "What? You kept talking about how cute he was." she shrugged, her eyes finding his face again. "She's shy." I felt like slapping her.

"Ah," he said, like he was unsure what else *to* say. Not that I blamed him.

"He's still waiting for your order," she reminded me with a wink. Begrudgingly, I ordered my frozen yogurt and moved out of the way.

Bethany paid for the yogurts. "Stay here and get our yogurt. I'm going to go find us some seats," she said and walked away.

I backed up, standing at the end of the counter where our orders would arrive. I glanced up, and saw that the boy Bethany had declared my infatuation for was putting my frozen treat together. He caught me staring. I looked away embarrassed.

He laughed. "You know, you don't have to be embarrassed about it." I really had no idea how to respond to that. "I've got friends who do the same thing."

"Yeah, friends," I laughed nervously. He grinned again, his dimples visible. He really was cute. He set the dishes on the counter.

"Thanks," I said softly, stepping up to grab the frozen treats.

"You're welcome. Come back sometime, Olivia," he said, sending a wink my way. The blush crept back into my cheeks as I turned away, biting my lip to keep the smile from appearing.

Bethany waved me over to the table she'd secured near the edge of the food courts. When I reached her, she frowned. "What?"

"You forgot spoons," she noted. Glancing down, I felt like smacking myself in the face. Of course I forgot spoons and would now have to go back and get some.

"I'll be right back." I set the frozen yogurt cups down and walked back to the shop to get spoons. The boy saw me coming, and like a psychic, handed me two spoons as I made it to the counter. "Thank you."

"No problem." He winked. I was going to turn into a tomato before I got home at this rate when it came to blushing.

While we ate our frozen yogurt, we people watched. Bethany gave guys ratings as they passed by. So far no one had rated above an eight. I personally thought it was degrading to be rated, but I had been subject to the last one picked when I was younger, so it was a sore spot.

"Oh, he's a ten!" she chimed, dipping her spoon in her remaining frozen yogurt. I raised an eyebrow and looked for the person she'd just rated. The guy from the yogurt stand came into view, his paper hat in hand.

"That's the first ten all afternoon. Why do you like him so much?" I moved my eyes back to her. She wore a small smile, her eyes still watching him. "Bethany?"

She shook her head, returning her attention to me. "There's just something about him. He seems like a likeable guy, and you need someone like that."

"You could use that, too," I mumbled, taking another bite of my melting yogurt.

"Hold the phone, is that what I think it is?" Bethany's brown gaze widened and a smile lit up her face.

"What?" I hated not knowing what she was talking about. She pointed and I twisted the frozen yogurt cup around in my hand. I gaped.

"Ten gave you his number."

I was in shock. This kind of thing never happened to me. She giggled, finishing her frozen yogurt. "Ten has a name. Ryan," I murmured, reading the messy hand writing.

"Call him!" she urged, clapping her hands.

"No, I could never," I said, setting the cup down. "He probably gave me that rejection number."

"Or his real one." She sat up straighter, looking around the crowd to see if he was still around. When she didn't find him, she turned back to me. "Do it for me. Call the cute boy." She clasped her hands, sticking her lower lip out.

"I don't know if that's a good idea." She grabbed her phone from the table and started dialing. "Bethany," I pleaded. She shoved the phone into my hands and glared until I put it against my ear. "I hate you." After a few moments, the phone picked up.

"Hello?" Ryan's deep voice echoed.

"Hi, um, it's Olivia." When he chuckled, I wanted to hang up and run away, hide away from civilization and accept my fate to be alone forever. Of course it was a joke. His co-workers probably put him up to it.

"I wondered if you would notice the number. When I walked by it didn't look like you had yet," he told me, calming my nerves. He wasn't making fun of me, or playing a joke.

"Oh, yeah."

"I'm glad you saw it though." I bit my lip, the smile breaking through anyways. "So, Olivia. Is there a reason you're calling? Or did you just miss the sound of my voice?"

"Well there was that," I agreed, a giggle escaping my lips.

"Understandable," he said. "If you're not busy right now, I don't have anything else to do. Would you wanna hang out? I know you're with your friend, and I don't want to interrupt that."

I covered the mouth piece. "He wants to hang out." Bethany nodded eagerly. I turned back to the phone. "That sounds like fun. When and where?"

He whistled. I jumped, turning in my seat to see him standing a few feet away, the phone pressed to his ear. He'd changed from his work clothes into dark blue straight leg jeans, and a red t-shirt. "Hey."

"Hi," I breathed, feeling familiar butterflies invade my stomach. His dark hair had been fluffed up like he had done it to regain some of the thickness he'd lost from wearing a hat all day.

He glanced at Bethany. "I'm Ryan Newly, just by the way." He flashed a smile.

"Bethany Bridges," she greeted back. She glanced my way, nodding toward him with a stealth wink that wasn't so stealthy considering the grin the spread across his features.

"Um, so," I started nervously. "What did you want to do? We don't really have any ideas."

"I don't know. I figured hanging out with cute girls would be a good start though." he flirted. Bethany and I exchanged glances of amusement. "But, I'm open to suggestions. There are movies, more shopping–" he grimaced. "And food. I'm open to whatever."

"Movies are always fun," I added, glancing at Bethany.

"I'll buy the popcorn," Ryan offered, running a hand through his hair, leaving pieces of hair pointed up in his wake.

"You're a smart man." Bethany smiled. "The way to a woman's heart is through your wallet," she quipped, a giggle escaping her lips.

"That's just Bethany," I clarified, standing from my seat.

"Yes, I'm a very selfish person," she agreed. "Let's just go see the movie. Ryan can learn about all of our bad habits later. We don't want to scare him off."

"I'm not an easy person to scare off, so don't worry." He winked. "Let's go. Movies aren't going to watch themselves," he said, extending his arm in the direction of the theater.

After the movie, we grabbed a late lunch. We talked and laughed like we'd known each other for a long time. I'd never been able to talk to someone so easily before, especially someone of the opposite sex.

I made sure to listen intently when he was talking about himself. I learned he was nineteen, graduated the year before. He was currently saving up money for a new car and he planned to follow in his father's footsteps and become a fireman. Most girls wanted a hero, and here I was sitting next to one.

"Alright, I've got to go. I need to help my dad with some things before it gets too dark," Ryan acknowledged, glancing up from his watch. "But I'd love to hang out again, if you guys don't feel creeped out by me." He gave a half-smile, like he wasn't sure of the answer he'd get.

"You're pretty chill so far," I assured him. "We'll definitely be calling to hang out."

"Awesome!" he cheered lightly, standing up. We followed his lead and all walked to our cars. He smiled, waving as he drove off.

As soon as he was out of the parking lot, Bethany turned to me. "What'd you think?" she demanded.

I laughed. "I just met him. Give me some time to let it sink in," I brushed off the question. I wasn't sure what I thought of him, honestly. He was cute, and seemed like a nice enough guy. But I knew it would be stupid to get in a relationship when I was still in love with someone else. It wouldn't be fair to Ryan.

"Are you serious?" she deadpanned. "He's cute, funny, and nice. What else do you need?" she threw her arms up in exasperation.

"You can go after him if you want, Bethany," I giggled.

"He likes you, I could see the way he was looking at you," she murmured, turning toward the car. Frowning, I headed after her. *And I saw the way you looked at him.*

Chapter Six – Monday Madness

I walked into class Monday morning, hoping the day would go by quickly. Bethany, Ryan, and I planned another outing after school. The weather was perfect for a trip to the beach. He planned to pick us up after school and then we'd all drive to the beach together and meet up with some of his friends. I was nervous to meet them, but he assured me they were cool and that we would all get along smashingly.

Lex and his friends had gotten together over the weekend at his house. They played loud music and yelled a lot. I assumed they were killing each other in video games. He had called to try and talk with me, but I refused when Mom told me who was on the phone. I didn't want to talk to him. Something had changed, and I knew whatever had changed wouldn't make my life any easier.

The teacher came in and we got to work on clauses, one of my least favorite parts of English. I sighed and turned my attention back to the front. I needed to know this stuff. I had a quiz coming up.

After class, I walked down towards the lunch room, found my normal table, and sat down. I pulled my lunch out of my bag and began eating, waiting for Bethany. She usually got out of class a little later than I did.

The sound of footsteps caused me to look up. My heart jumped in my chest. "What do you want?"

"Can we talk?" Lex asked. People glanced across the room curiously. He usually didn't talk to me unless there was a crowd.

"I was pretty sure I made myself clear when I refused to talk to you all weekend," I muttered, taking a bite of my peanut butter and jelly sandwich.

"Come on. I need to talk with you," he continued.

I shook my head. "No. I'm not going to talk to you. Not after what happened."

"Honeybee, please." He whispered to me. His dark green irises almost looked sincere. *Almost.*

I wanted to believe him. But the heartache I felt wouldn't let me. I couldn't set myself up for more heartbreak. Doing so without realizing it was one thing, but to knowingly walk back to him would kill me.

"Please leave, Lex."

"Not until you say you'll talk to me." He held his ground.

"I'm asking nicely," I pointed out.

He scoffed, crossing his arms over his chest. "I obviously don't care. I want to talk with you."

"Not now," I growled.

"Later then?" he questioned. I threw my hands up in exasperation. He sure was persistent.

"I'm not promising anything. I have plans for later," I answered.

"I'll come over tonight," he told me. "See you then." He left the table just as Bethany came over. I felt a weight on my shoulders. Why couldn't he just leave me alone?

Bethany glared at his retreating back before sitting down. "What was that about?"

"He wants to talk," I pouted, glaring at my sandwich.

"I hope you said no." She frowned.

"I did. But he said he's coming over later, anyways," I grumbled.

"Don't let yourself be sweet talked into forgiving him," she warned. I nodded. No way was I letting him sweet talk his way back into my heart. "A few more hours and we'll be leaving for the beach."

"I literally can't wait." I glanced up as I saw someone make their way over towards us. "Don't look now, but your fiancée is coming over." She turned and glanced at Jeremiah as he walked over. He set his food down next to her and smiled over at me.

"Jeremiah," she said less than enthusiastically. She wasn't sold on the idea that he actually liked her. Part of her still felt he was just doing it to watch her fall. "Hey girls," he turned towards Bethany. "Where did you go on Friday?" he asked.

"Olivia and I had plans," she told him. "I'm sorry I couldn't wait longer." She gave a small smile.

"No worries, I was just worried when you were gone," he replied.

"That's so sweet," I cooed. Bethany shot a glance my way.

"I'm a sweet guy," he chimed in, an arrogant grin on his face. *Yeah, maybe not.* He turned back to her. "Anyways, I still have that thing for you. I can bring it to math class."

"Sure." She nodded. There was an awkward tension between the two of them, but it didn't look like Jeremiah noticed that.

"Want to walk to class together?" he winked, resting his arms on the table.

"Not today," she replied easily. His carefree smile dropped from his face. "Olivia and I have to talk a little longer."

"Oh," he sighed, his eyes dropping. "I'll let you guys talk then…" he trailed off, standing and moving away from the table.

"You're such a heartbreaker, Bethany," I chided, clucking my tongue at her.

"It happens to the best of us." She shrugged. She glanced at the clock on the main wall. "I really should get to class."

"Same." I picked up my garbage. "I'll see you in homeroom," I told her. She nodded, walking off. After throwing my garbage away, I went to my next class.

After school ended, I waited outside for Bethany. Ryan had texted me saying he would be there soon. He was picking up a few other people. That part made me even more nervous. I didn't like the idea of making small talk for an hour long drive with people I didn't know.

The warm breeze caressed my skin, bringing a wave of calm to my mind. Part of why I loved California was because the warm weather had a way of calming my mood. I was ninety percent sure that if I was to move somewhere cold and wet, I would suffer from Seasonal Affective Disorder.

A dark green car pulled up to the curb. Ryan was in the front seat, another boy and girl were in the car with him. The girl was in the backseat, and the other guy was riding shot gun. The engine turned off and Ryan got out of the car. He waved over the hood before walking over to me.

"Hey," I smiled up at him.

"Hey, cutie." He winked. "Where is your friend?" he glanced around.

I chuckled, standing up. "Probably trying to get out of her math class."

He raised an eyebrow. "Trying?"

"She gets held up a lot," I explained, pulling my backpack over my shoulder.

"We should go find her then," he decided, nodding his head as if to answer his own question. He glanced at my backpack. "Want to put that in the trunk?"

"Sure." I followed him over to the car and deposited my backpack in the trunk. A door opened and the boy stepped out of the car. He was tall, and kind of lanky. Sunglasses hid his eyes from view, and his red hair blazed in the sun.

"Oh, right." Ryan snapped his fingers. "Billy, this is Olivia. Olivia, this is Billy." The car window rolled down, and the girl stuck her head out. Gray eyes smiled up at me, and brown bangs covered her forehead. "And this is Grace."

She smiled, sticking her hand out to me. "I'm Billy's twin sister." I did a double take. They both had pale skin, but that seemed to be the only thing they had in common. "Not identical," she added with a laugh.

"That makes way more sense," I replied.

Ryan grinned. "We're going to go find Bethany, we'll be back soon."

"Fine. But leave the keys? She's texting her boyfriend and I have nothing to do," Billy mumbled. Ryan tossed him the keys, and then gestured for me to lead the way.

I walked back down the walkway, Ryan right behind me. The cologne he wore smelled fantastic. The black board shorts and green t-shirt looked good on him, showing off his tan skin and muscles.

"So how was your day at school?" he glanced over at me, dark bangs falling into his eyes.

"It was okay," I replied, shrugging. He nudged my shoulder. I glanced around quickly to make sure there wasn't a pair of ears listening that would spread rumors. "Long story short, the guy I've been in love with for a while is making life more complicated."

He frowned. "How is he making it worse?"

I played with the ends of my hair. "He kind of kissed me while he was dating someone else, and then told me it was a mistake. Which, I mean, I guess it was, but it still hurts."

He dropped an arm around my shoulder. "Love hurts." I nodded. "But don't worry, there's someone out there for you. If it isn't this guy, it'll be someone better," he promised.

"Thanks, Ryan," I smiled up at him, hugging him around the waist.

"My pleasure."

Ahead of us, a door opened. Bethany sure took her sweet time getting out of that classroom. I looked over with a bright smile. "Bethan-"

"Honeybee?" Lex's eyes moved from me to Ryan, who still had his arm around me. Lex narrowed his eyes and looked back at me.

"Lex," I uttered. Ryan seemed to realize Lex was the boy I was talking about, and his body tensed beside me.

"What are you still doing here?" His eyes lingered on Ryan's arm, still perched on my shoulder.

"Waiting for Bethany," I mumbled. *Why did I feel guilty?*

"What's it to you?" Ryan questioned, raising an eyebrow.

"And you are?" Lex crossed his arms defensively.

"I'm her boy friend," Ryan answered easily. *My what?*

"Her what?" Lex bit out. *He was upset?* Why would he be upset?

"Her boy friend," Ryan repeated, raising his eyebrows. "You do know what that means right?"

Lex turned his glare to me. "So this is the real reason you didn't want to talk to me?" he rolled his eyes. "And you think I'm bad," he muttered.

"Don't talk to her like that," Ryan warned.

"Don't tell me what to do, man. Pretty sure I've known her longer than you have," Lex muttered.

"Pretty sure that doesn't matter right now," he pointed out, smirking. The door behind Lex opened, and Bethany's head appeared. "Bethany!" Ryan smiled. "We're ready to go."

She looked at Ryan and me, her gaze flickering over to Lex in question. "Okay." She walked around the seething blond and reached us.

"It was great to meet you, Lex." Ryan beamed before turned around and walking away. We quickly followed after him, not wanting to be caught in Lex's anger.

Before Bethany could ask any questions of her own, I asked mine first. "Did Jeremiah give you the gift he was talking about?"

She glared, knowing that I was stalling. "Yeah. It was a pair of earrings."

"Who's Jeremiah?" Ryan asked, slipping his sunglasses over his eyes.

"Her secret admirer who isn't secretive."

"He's not my admirer. I'm pretty sure he's just messing with me," she mumbled. "Now! What was that about?"

"I was just being a cool dude," Ryan assured her. "Nothing to worry about."

"You told him you were my boyfriend," I blurted. Bethany's eyes widened.

"I did tell him that," he admitted. "But if I had told him that in writing, all of you would've seen the space in between the word boy and the word friend. I bet you all feel silly for just assuming there wasn't a space." He winked, with a crooked grin on his face.

I groaned. "Ryan."

"What, I'm being helpful. Making a guy jealous is one of the fastest ways to get them to admit their feelings, if to no one else then at least to themselves, which usually leads to telling the girl," he told me. He looked so sure of himself. Oh if only he knew what he'd just done. Lex didn't react the same ways other guys would have. His first reaction was to run. Or, like when we were younger, he would tell my mom.

"He's not going to get jealous and tell me he likes me. He's going to get angry and tell my mom." Ryan's smile dropped.

"Seriously?" I looked up, startled to see Billy leaning against the car, not only listening to our conversation, but adding to it.

"Yeah." I sighed.

"I'm sorry, I didn't know," Ryan apologized. "Maybe I can fix this."

"There's not much you can do now anyways. I'll just ignore my phone until we get home from the beach," I told them.

"A day at the beach fixes everything," Billy smiled, sliding back into the car. Ryan shot me one more look of regret before he moved to the driver's seat. Bethany and I got into the car, sitting in the back with Grace.

Hopefully Lex wouldn't fall into old ways, and the beach would wash away my worries. There was far too much drama in my life for someone who didn't have that many friends and had never been on a date.

Chapter Seven – Pillows M.I.A

At the beach, we met the rest of Ryan's friends. There was a couple; Rick and Noelle. Rick was blond, with light blue eyes. His height loomed over Noelle, who was short with brown hair and eyes. There was also Aaron, who was dating Grace. He had dark brown hair, and looked like someone who went to the gym a lot.

They were all like Ryan; friendly and fun to be around. I completely forgot about the problem with Mom until we reached my driveway. Bethany put the car in park, and we both stared at the house. The lights were on, and Mom's car was in the driveway.

"You want to come over to my house instead?" she offered. It was better to get it out of the way now instead of prolong the inevitable. With a sigh, I shook my head and unbuckled. I pulled my bag from the backseat and got out of the car.

"Good luck."

"Thanks, I'm going to need it." I swallowed hard.

"Go get em', tiger," she encouraged, waving before she drove home.

With a deep breath, I started up toward the front door. I glanced back at Lex's house, sad to see his car was there and he was likely home, too. The sliver of hope I had that he would be gone and Mom wouldn't know about Ryan vanished.

As soon as I opened the door I heard her talking. She was in the kitchen, and probably on the phone. A spark of hope ignited inside me. *She's distracted*! I made a dash for the stairs, hoping to retire to my room for a while.

"Livie, is that you?" she called out.

My shoulders slumped, and I moped back down the stairs, heading into the kitchen. "Yeah." I stepped into the kitchen. Mom was leaning against the counter, and there was no phone in sight. That wasn't a good sign. Who had she been talking to?

"Hey," Lex's voice caused me to jump. He sneered at my reaction.

"What are you doing here?" I hissed, my heart still rapidly beating against my chest. Of course he was the one she was talking to. Why couldn't he leave me alone? It was bad enough I had to deal with him at school, and in the outside world. Even my tree house wasn't safe from his presence. Home was supposed to be my place of rest, not another place he could torment me in.

"I told you I was coming over earlier," he reminded. I'd hoped he would forget about that.

"Did you eat?" Mom asked.

I nodded slowly, tearing my eyes away from Lex. "We ate on the way home."

"Ah, yes. You and your new friend Ryan," she said, giving me a pointed look. I smiled nervously beneath her blue eyes. "Lex, would you give us a minute?"

He nodded, standing to move past me. I saw the look of satisfaction in those dark green orbs as he passed. His heavy footsteps on the stairs worried me. *What is he doing upstairs?*

"Olivia," Mom murmured.

I bit my lip. "It got out of hand. Ryan was just being protective of me."

The words fell from my lips quickly as I told her about what Ryan had said, and what had happened. She knew about my feelings for Lex. After Dad died, she was the only person I could confide in about boys, like the one across the street. She never told me not to like him, which made me think that maybe Lex had a point about Patty and Mom planning our future.

"Okay," she murmured, nodding her head. "I understand why he did it. Ryan sounds like a nice young man." She brushed her brown hair from her eyes. "And who knows, maybe there will be something between you two in the future." Emotion sparked in her eyes.

"Maybe," I said slowly, not totally sure why she'd said that. I wasn't going to start dating anyone until I could get over Lex. No one deserved to be second best in their own relationship. "I'm going to go upstairs and kick Lex out."

"Holler if you need anything," she said, kissing my cheek as she took a platter with a salad and bowl of soup on it into the living room.

"I will."

I walked up the stairs, glancing at the pictures that had been on the wall since I was little. Mom and Dad's wedding picture, my first birthday, a picture from a vacation we took to Disneyland. The Mickey Mouse ears on top of Dad's head made him look all the more goofy. At the top of the stairs was one of the last pictures we'd taken before Dad's accident. In the picture he was teaching me how to play baseball. Lex was in the picture too, standing beside me with a black glove instead of the pink one I had. I bit my lip at the sudden swing of emotion and moved past the memories that lingered on the wall.

When I stepped into my room, Lex was sitting at my desk. He was texting on his phone, feet propped up on the top of the desk. I frowned but didn't say anything. Moving to my bed, I laid down, my face turned away from him. Maybe he didn't even know I was in there with him. The chair hit the desk, he was probably standing up. I could hear him coming closer to the bed.

"You know, it's rude to go into someone's room without knocking," I mumbled, fully aware that I hadn't been in my room when he walked in. But that almost made it worse.

"Knocking is for losers," he said, sitting down on the bed and scooting closer to me. I didn't move. He reached over and pushed my leg, causing me to jerk. "Honeybee, take your face out of your pillow. It's hard to talk to someone who isn't even looking at me."

"Why should I?" I muttered. It was hard to breathe when a pillow was over my face, but I wasn't going to give in and look at him just yet.

"Honeybee, I want to talk to you about last weekend," he sighed. "I feel…" he paused. I raised an eyebrow against my pillow. Was Lex Diamond actually going to admit feeling bad about what he did? "We've known each other too long to just stop talking."

Nope.

"We hardly ever talked as it was." I turned over in my bed, taking in a breath, and looked up at him. "You can go now."

"Not until you talk to me." He was so stubborn.

"I am talking to you." I grumbled, watching a smile capture his lips. Just thinking about his lips made my mind replay the kiss. How could kissing him feel so right when he didn't care?

"Yeah, but you're not responding the way I want you to," he replied.

"The world doesn't revolve around you, Lex," I retorted.

He smiled, grabbing my foot. "That's what you think, but the rest of the world knows what's what."

I kicked his hand away. "Shut up."

"Whoa, you're getting kind of feisty. I don't know if your boyfriend will like that," he cautioned.

I raised my eyebrows. "Do I detect a hint of annoyance in your voice?"

"No, you do not," he promised.

"I think I do. You're annoyed that I have a boyfriend." I challenged, letting the lie drag out a little longer. What could it hurt?

He just smiled at me. "You have no idea what you're talking about." I stuck my tongue out at him and turned my face back down onto my pillow. He got up off of my bed. I smiled, thinking he was leaving.

Yeah right.

He lay down on my bed next to me, pushing me over so he'd have more room.

"Lex!" I groaned, fighting the urge to smother him with a pillow and be done with him forever. Not only was he stronger than me, but I would never hold up in the court of law. They would see right through my lies. I could always plead insanity. What court wouldn't believe he'd driven me insane?

"It's been a long time since we've done this," he said, ignoring me.

"Done what?" I asked.

"Slept in the same bed," he replied.

"We're not sleeping," I noted dryly.

He slapped my leg gently. "Shut up, you know what I meant."

"I do. I think it's because I've known you for far too long," I mumbled, sitting up and leaning against the headboard. I glanced down at him, his hands rested on his abdomen, lifting with each breath.

"It's been traumatizing to know you this long." He opened one eye and looked at me.

"You think you were traumatized? You have no idea," I retorted.

"Oh be quiet. You were plenty traumatizing," he said with a grin.

"How?" I gasped.

"Like when I walked in on you half naked," he said. I shuddered inwardly in remembrance. I'd been in shorts and a bra when he'd barged in. I was lucky my shock didn't keep me frozen for too long and I'd pulled a shirt on pretty quickly. We didn't speak for two days after that.

"You were the one who kept staring at me. You could've looked away," I reminded him.

"Yeah, but it was like a deer in the headlights, I couldn't look away." He turned on his side, propped up on his elbow.

I rolled my eyes. "You kept looking because you're a pervert."

"I am not," he replied. "I was curious thirteen year old, there's a difference."

"Not even." I sighed. "And I'm mad at you still, so will you please leave?"

"We still haven't talked about the tree house," he reminded me.

"I don't want to talk about the tree house. Not now, and not ever. Can't we just pretend it never happened? You do that so well," I hissed.

"If we don't talk about it, you'll be mad at me forever," he sat up, leaning against the backboard so we were at the same level.

"I have good reason to be mad at you forever." I glared. "You keep kissing me and then running away. I'm tired of being the person you mess with when you're bored."

"I wasn't messing with you. What's wrong with a couple of good looking friends making out once in a while?" he asked. I rolled my eyes. He complimented me, but he still came off sounding like a pig.

"Do I really need to explain why?" I asked. "It would be cheating on our significant others."

"Minor details."

"Your girlfriend is not a minor detail!" I shoved him off the bed, anger rising in my chest. "Leave." He stood and dropped his face near mine. *He is seconds away from being slapped.*

"What's the magic word?"

I pushed a pillow in his face. "You don't respond to the magic word. Now get out before I slap you."

He sighed and stood up, tossing the pillow back at me. "Fine, I'll leave. But we are talking about this. You live across the street. You're not going to avoid me that easily." He smiled. I threw the pillow at him angrily. He caught it, which annoyed me more.

"Bye, Honeybee," he said exiting the room. I stared at the door for a few seconds, waiting for the annoyance to subside.

Then it struck me.

"He just took my pillow." I mumbled to myself. I sighed and rolled over onto my stomach, and screamed into my remaining pillows.

I was in love with the devil. The insanity plea would definitely work.

Chapter Eight – Nothing Short of Curious

I got home from school the next day and Mom was in the process of setting up the backyard for the get together. She had informed me earlier the Diamond's were coming over for dinner and I was supposed to invite my friends over, which was Mom code for: Lex told his mom about Ryan, and she wants to meet him.

Her gaze found me as I stood right outside the door. "Hey, Mom." I waved.

"Hey, sweetie." she looked back at the table, setting down the final pieces of pale yellow plastic utensils. "How was school?"

I shrugged, stepping out into the lawn. The lush green grass was soft beneath my bare feet. Mr. Diamond, or occasionally Lex, came over and tended to our lawn every couple weeks. It was a sweet gesture; one Mom seemed to appreciate a lot. "It was fine, as usual. How was your day?"

"Oh you know how it goes." She laughed, pushing her hair behind her ear. "Forward some emails, answer phones, get signatures on documents. The same old thing I do every day." I could tell by the way she talked she wanted to be somewhere else, doing something else. She never liked the hustle and bustle of the law firm.

"Sounds like fun."

She frowned before looking back at me. "What time are your friends coming over?"

"I told them to come over a little earlier. That way they would just be here and not have to be introduced later. So six thirty," I answered. I knew it was only four, so we still had a few hours to get everything ready.

"Is Ryan going to come?" she questioned, setting up the lawn decorations. She had a few gnomes and a plastic deer that linger in the back corner, opposite the tree house. Whenever I slept in the tree house in the summers, I would wake up sometimes and see the gnomes staring back at me, evil little smiles plastered on their evil little faces. Talk about traumatic. I wasn't sure if there was a phobia for gnomes, but if there was, I probably had it.

"Yeah," I remembered to answer. The conversation with Ryan had been less intimidating than I'd originally thought. He actually felt guilty about starting the rumor that I had a boyfriend, and had immediately agreed to come help me out. I was pretty sure he just wanted to mess with Lex more, but I didn't care. Lex could hold his own. "He's agreed to come. I warned him of who all was coming."

"Wonderful!" she smiled, clasping her hands together. "I've got to finish making dinner. The back yard is set up. If you could be a dear, clean up the living room and downstairs bathroom. I'm going to assume they won't go upstairs and hope for the best," she said more to herself than me.

"Will do," I promised, saluting her. She laughed and waved me away. I moved back inside the house and started to tidy up the house. Smells of dinner wafted into the living room as I cleaned. Dinner was going to be good.

Once everything had been tidied up, and Mom gave me freedom to do as I wished until my friends came over, I took a shower and started to get ready. I wasn't entirely sure what to wear, but I was hopeful that I would find something cute to impress the young men in attendance. Even though I wasn't interested in a relationship with Ryan,

I could still look cute. Cute boys made my day brighter. I could only hope the same thing could be said about guys seeing cute girls.

I pulled on a short teal dress with thick straps and white flowers stitched across the bottom right of the skirt. I fish tailed may hair, putting on minimal makeup and then slipped on my glasses. My favorite shoes were on my feet, the familiar black and tan animal print were a good blend with the bright dress.

The doorbell rang, bringing forth a cringe. No doubt Mom would answer the door before I even made it out of my bedroom. I prayed to God it was Bethany at the door, and not Ryan. Moving from my room, I made my way toward the staircase. My heartbeat sped up when Ryan's dark mop appeared through the doorway.

"It's so nice to meet you," Mom greeted, smiling. "Olivia told me how you pretended to be her boyfriend."

Ryan chuckled, rubbing the back of his neck. "Yeah, that wasn't my brightest idea."

The moment of distraction gave me enough time to take in his appearance. It seemed he'd dressed up a bit for the get together. Who he was trying to impress, I didn't know. He wore a dark green polo and tan shorts. Casual tennis shoes claimed his feet, and a silver watch sparkled on his wrist. He looked good. *Really* good.

"Olivia is just getting changed upstairs," she told him, gesturing toward the staircase. Knowing I would be found staring, I started down the steps. Mom looked up. "Oh, there she is now. Hon, your friend is here."

"I can see that." I nodded, getting to the bottom of the steps. "Hey, Ryan." He waved, a smile gracing his lips. The glittering of the overhead light on his lips caught my attention. Almost unconsciously, his tongue prodded the ring on his lower lip. "I like it," I decided.

Ryan's grin widened. "Well, I did get it to impress the girls." Mom raised an eyebrow at the two of us but didn't say anything. "When is everyone else getting here?"

"In about a half an hour," I informed him. "Bethany should be here before then, though. She said she would, at least." He nodded, glancing around the house. "Want a tour?" I bit my lip.

"Absolutely." He nodded, brushing hair out of his eyes.

Looking closer, I could see the specks of blue in his dark brown eyes. They reminded me of the hazel and gold drops in Lex's eyes. I cursed myself inwardly for thinking of Lex and his eyes. They were practically my kryptonite. "Great."

"Great," he mimicked, chuckling.

"I'll be in the kitchen," Mom said, smiling before excusing herself.

I waved a hand toward the living room, very aware of how close he followed behind me. I bit my lip again, and walked ahead. "This is the living room. I come in here to gorge on ice cream and watch movies on the weekends. And occasionally the weekdays, too."

"Good to know." He pursed his lips, walking over to the bookshelf. The shelves were lined with lots of Dad's old books, Mom's new books, and pictures of the family. "Is your dad here?" he glanced back at me.

The familiar pang filled my heart. Most of the time, it didn't hurt. But when I explained to people what happened, the pity in their eyes for the girl who grew up without a dad hurt to see. The looks always reminded me that I had lost someone special. "No," I answered.

"Too bad," he sighed, turning back to face me. "I would've liked to have met him."

I forced a smile. "He died when I was twelve, killed in a hit and run accident." His eyes instantly dimmed, his lips parting as he started to apologize. Apologies got so tiring. Was there nothing else to say then 'I'm sorry'? "Don't," I stopped him. "You didn't know, and you don't have to apologize. It's been a long time."

"I don't really know what to say then," he murmured, his lips curling downward.

My face twisted, wrinkling my nose and lips to one side. "You don't have to say anything," I breathed. "Come on. I'll show you a few more rooms, and then we can go outside and hangout until Bethany comes." His eyes regained some of their lightheartedness, and he nodded.

We were outside sitting on one of the benches, enjoying the last bit of time we had left. Soon enough, Lex would come, bringing his *lovely* girlfriend. Admittedly, I was a little excited to see what she did when she saw my 'boyfriend'.

A little before seven, Bethany showed up. She looked as good as always, wearing a white dress and yellow cardigan. Before I was ready, the doorbell rang again. With a deep breath, I moved to answer it. Ryan and Bethany stood nearby, chatting in the living room. I pulled open the door and smiled brightly at Patty and Steve. Lex and Cassy were behind them, shooting glares at each other.

"Hey," I greeted.

"Olivia!" Patty smiled warmly at me. She opened her arms and gave me a hug. Once she let go, her eyes traveled behind me. "And you must be Ryan?"

He stepped up beside me, shaking her hand. "Yes, I am. It's nice to meet you, Mrs. Diamond."

"Please, call me, Patty," she said, moving forward and allowing the other three to come in as well. Steve smiled politely, shaking Ryan's hand before following his wife further into the house.

Cassy's eyes left Lex and gleamed in delight upon seeing Ryan. I bit my lip to keep my nasty remark to myself. "I'm Cassy," she breathed, pushing her chest out.

"Ryan." He nodded curtly. The disappointment in Cassy's eyes was evident, but she quickly moved on, slipping her hand into Lex's. He held her hand limply, nodding to me as he shut the door behind him. The two of them walked into the kitchen, Lex nodding in Bethany's direction. She gave a small wave.

"You didn't mention that particular Cassy was coming," Ryan mumbled. My heart seemed to stop. They'd acted like they didn't know each other, but what if they had been together in the past? "I'm pretty sure she's sleeping with one of the guys at work."

I turned on him, eyes wide. "But she's with Lex." I glanced toward the kitchen. Cassy leaned against Lex, but he seemed void of emotion toward her. She looked up at him, pushing her lower lip out and giving him the puppy dog eyes. His face was stone cold as he glanced down at her, eyes hardening. "I wonder if he knows…"

"If he considers their relationship to be exclusive, then he probably doesn't know. Nor is he going to like when he finds out," Ryan gave a grim smile.

Bethany groaned, parting her hair. "For our sake, I hope he doesn't find out tonight."

Me too.

Mom moved out of the kitchen, pointing at the three of us. "Food is ready. We're all going to dish up and go outside." She disappeared back into the kitchen. I wasn't entirely sure what we were having for dinner. I knew there was a salad, and something had been in the over earlier.

Ryan headed in first, Bethany and I trailed behind him. "Wow, this all looks really good, Debby."

Mom smiled her thanks, and turned to me. "Make sure your friends know where everything is."

I saluted. "Yes ma'am." I glanced over, and realization hit me. Salmon for dinner, that explained the fish smell. Mom walked outside. I could see that everyone else was outside, leaving just us three to get our food.

"So, this should be fun, huh?" Bethany joked, glancing at the two of us. I was a bit nervous about the conversations that would no doubt come up. Ryan and I hadn't even talked about our backstory. I would probably be mute most of the night to avoid giving away our lack of a love story.

"So much fun." Ryan winked, putting food on his plate.

I followed suit, and soon we were all walking out of the house and toward the picnic table where everyone else sat. Lex and Cassy sat together. He still seemed to be angry with her for unknown reasons.

The three of us sat down at the table. Ryan sat in between Bethany and I, my mom and the Diamond's sitting on either side of us, with Lex and Cassy on the opposite side. Everyone started eating, commenting on how good the food was, and talking generally about their days.

Before long, the questioning began.

"So, Olivia, how did you and Ryan meet?" Patty asked.

"We met at the frozen yogurt place in the mall," I answered. Cassy's features hardened, almost in fear. She looked away from Ryan.

"Oh, how cute," Patty crooned, sending a smile toward Mom.

Ryan smiled at me before he added in. "You think that's cute? Babe, you should tell her about our first conversation." *Babe*? We'd talked a little bit about playing the part, and acting like we were going out. But I hadn't realized pet names were part of that.

"What do you mean?" I questioned.

"You know," he started, "Bethany had to tell me you thought I was cute because you were too shy to tell me, then I put my number on your yogurt cup?"

"Did he really?" Cassy smiled. She'd never smiled at me before.

"Yeah," I replied slowly, unsure of why she was acting interested.

"Oh, that's so adorable!" She cooed. "Lex, how come you don't do anything cute like that?"

"Maybe I would if you weren't constantly throwing yourself at other guys," he said casually. My jaw dropped at his words, and the rest of the table seemed to have a similar reaction. What was his problem?

Cassy blushed. "Lex."

"You're the one who asked," he told her. She frowned and turned away from him. I took another bite of my salmon, watching the tension between Lex and Cassy rise.

"So, Ryan, where do you go to high school?" Mom smiled, breaking the silence.

"I'm out of high school actually," he answered.

Lex caught my eye, raising an eyebrow as if he was secretly judging my choice of boyfriend. Like he could really judge me on the boys I dated.

Patty raised her eyebrows. "Oh? Are you going to college somewhere?"

"Not yet." Ryan shot me a glance. Had he not expected the conversation to go toward his education? He obviously never met any of the families of his previous girlfriends.

"You're young," Patty shrugged. "What do your parents do?"

"My mom doesn't work, and my dad is a retired fireman." He replied, taking a sip of his soda.

"Any siblings?" Mom asked.

Ryan smiled charmingly. "No, why? Do you have more children who are in need of a great…" he trailed off, looking at me.

"Boyfriend," I filled.

He grinned at me, snapping his fingers and extending his index finger my way. "Yes."

Mom laughed. "No, I just curious. If you two get married, I want to have you at my house for the Holidays, not some sibling's house." Ryan's cheeks burned brightly with embarrassment.

"Planning ahead again are we?" I laughed.

"I'm a planner." She winked. Ryan shifted in his seat, the smile seemingly forced. She leaned over and patted his hand. "Don't worry, Ryan. I won't plan the wedding till she has a ring on her finger."

This time it was Lex who choked on his soda. Cassy glanced at him momentarily before returning to her food. Lex continued to cough for a minute or so before regaining his composure.

"Are you alright?" Patty finally asked.

"Whatever," he mumbled.

"The thought of me being married to someone handsome is hard for him to believe," I answered. Lex glared at me. I shrugged my shoulders carelessly.

"Who said he was handsome?" Lex asked.

I smiled sweetly at Ryan before turning back to Lex. "I did. My mom is probably trying to figure out what our kids are going to look like, and your parents don't seem to think he's ugly. Plus, you seem to dislike him for no reason, which aims to say you're intimidated by him."

Lex scoffed, swallowing more of his soda. "Who says someone like this guy could intimidate me?"

"I did. Weren't you listening?" I sighed.

"I freaking hate Bridges. She's turned you evil," he grumbled, glancing at Bethany who glared back at him, undaunted.

"Lex," Steve bit out the warning.

"And who do we have to blame for turning you evil?" I muttered. Bethany covered her mouth, laughter in her eyes.

"Olivia!" Mom snapped. I pressed my lips together to quench the laughter ready to spill out, and avoided looking at Bethany. If we met eyes both of us would lose it. She really had trained me to be a bit more evil. I would have to thank her for that later, being able to stand up against others was something I'd never really been able to do.

Steve shook his head, setting his fork down. "So, Ryan, you work at a frozen yogurt place?"

Ryan nodded. "Yes, sir. But I'm not planning on working for a yogurt stand the rest of my life, obviously." "Then what do you plan on doing?" Steve reached for his cup, taking a drink of water.

"I'm hoping to follow in my dad's footsteps and become a firefighter," Ryan replied. My heart melted. It was so sweet he wanted to follow his dad. I wondered what kind of career options Dad would've wanted for me.

"That's a very noble career choice," Steve said with a smile.

Lex rolled his eyes. "I'd follow my dad's footsteps, but he doesn't have what one would call a *noble* profession." Steve glared at Lex, who shrugged innocently. "What? Last time I checked, you still make women chestier, skinnier, and all around trashy." He rolled his eyes. "Plastic surgery is a joke."

"Plastic surgery gives hope to a lot of people. I don't only work on women who want enhancements," Steve growled. "Or did you forget that burn victims get plastic surgery as well?"

"Yeah, but how often does that really happen?" Lex glared at Steve. Patty glanced at Mom, then back to Steve and Lex. It looked like she was trying to figure out how to intervene before something bad went down between the two men. Lex and Steve had been at odds with each other for a while. I didn't know what happened, but it was obvious something had.

It hurt my heart to see kids and their dads not working through things, and falling away from each other. I didn't even get to know my dad in my teen years, he was gone so soon.

"Lex," I murmured calmly. His blazing green gaze turned on me, cutting through me. "You're being rude."

"No more than normal," he muttered, dropping his fork onto the plate with a loud clank. Cassy looked over at him, raising an eyebrow. He turned to Mom, a bright smile on his face. "Thanks for dinner, Debby. It was delicious." He pushed his chair back, and then started pulling out Cassy's chair for her. She seemed startled, dropping her fork onto to the plate, her food half uneaten.

"Where are you going?" Patty sighed, resting her chin in her hand.

"Out." Lex didn't offer any further explanation. "Honeybee, why don't you walk us to the door?" His glare made it clear I didn't really have a choice in the matter.

I excused myself and the three of us walked back into the house and toward the front door. Lex walked briskly, pausing at the door for us. He glanced at Cassy. "Go to the car, I'll be there in a minute." Her eyes met mine briefly before she left.

"Lex-"

"Stop acting like we're still five." His voice was cold. "We're not. You need to realize that we've both changed. I'm not the same guy you grew up with."

"Oh trust me, I've noticed," I muttered.

He frowned. "We're not little kids anymore, Olivia." My breath hitched in my chest. He *never* called me by my real name. It was Honeybee or bust. "So stop treating me like we're the same kids, playing house. I'm getting sick and tired of it."

My eyes, which had been staring at the ground, snapped up. "I'm getting sick of you being a jerk! You just disrespected your dad, and you're treating your girlfriend badly." I shook my head. "If you don't like her, you don't have to date her, but don't treat her that way."

He scoffed, crossing his arms. "When do you know anything about relationships? Ms. Forever Alone," he taunted. "This thing with the frozen yogurt boy isn't going to last, not when he has eyes for your best friend."

What? "I know about friendship," I faltered, unnerved by his words. "You don't treat your friends like crap, or you lose them. If you keep acting like everyone is beneath you, you're going to end up alone. Not even Cassy will put up with you forever."

"Gee, thanks," he sneered.

"You used to care about your friendships, about the people in your life," I mumbled. "I miss that." I turned away, heading back inside.

"I still care," his words came in a whisper. My eyes searched for his, but he'd already started across the street toward his car where Cassy was waiting. Sighing, I went inside to rejoin the party.

Chapter Nine – Distant Memories

After everyone went home, Bethany, Ryan, and I moved to the living room. Mom cleaned up the kitchen and retired to her room, sending us a look that said to be quiet and behave, or else. I got that look a lot lately.

"So, that was fun," Bethany mumbled, sipping a soda from the couch opposite of the one I was on.

"Totally," I sighed, twisting the hair that had escaped my braid. Ryan was sitting on the other end of the couch, his back was against the armrest and his legs were stretched out far enough that I could almost touch them. "Are you going to continue to be my friend after tonight?"

He grinned, nudging me with his foot. "You really think I'm that bad of a friend that I would leave after being interrogated by your family?" I shrugged. "Ouch."

"Sorry," I cooed, patting his leg.

"You guys totally looked like a couple tonight, by the way," Bethany blurted. I froze momentarily, not sure if that was a good thing or a bad thing.

"I'm actually an actor she hired," Ryan offered. I rolled my eyes, a grin slipping onto my face.

"I knew it." Bethany shot a glance my way. "So, are we going to talk about what happened between you and Lex tonight?" Ryan's head swiveled toward me.

"Which part?" I groaned, taking my braid out and shaking my hair out. I shivered, slipping the band around my wrist.

"When he asked you to walk them out," Ryan filled. Bethany nodded her agreement.

I didn't really want to talk about it, but it appeared I didn't have a choice. The words flew from my lips in a brief explanation of what had transpired when Lex left. Bethany pursed her lips, shooting reciprocated glances at Ryan. I adjusted on the couch, my legs stretching out on the couch, brushing Ryan's. "That's what happened."

They were silent for a few moments, still having a silent conversation via pointed looks. Finally, Ryan spoke. "Are you okay?"

I nodded stiffly. "Yeah, I'm … fine."

Bethany groaned, rolling her eyes. "Olivia, give it to us straight. Are you okay?" The look in her eyes told me she knew I wasn't. I couldn't count how many times I'd cried to her over Lex; something he'd done or said to me. She was subject to far too many breakdowns due to Lex and my stupidity.

My eyes fell to the floor. "No." Bethany frowned, again having a silent conversation with Ryan. I thought her and I had secret conversations, not her and Ryan.

"You're way out of his league," Ryan said, giving a small smile. "He doesn't deserve you."

I frowned, pulling my knees up to my chest. "Then why does it feel like it's the other way around?" I rested my chin on my knees. "I miss the old him, the *real* him."

"Maybe the real Lex is there, deep down," Bethany shrugged, ever hopeful for the love she disapproved of.

"What was he like before?" Ryan questioned, propping up on his elbows.

I laughed, remembering the Lex before popularity became his mission. "He was a total nerd. He needed glasses, and his favorite subject was math. He wanted to be an astronaut, and he had the biggest crush on Tinker Bell when we were little. Yet he still judged the fact I liked Peter Pan. He played soccer because he enjoyed it, not because it got him the popular vote."

"Old Lex was more fun," Bethany chimed in. "Not that I would know. I didn't get here in time."

"A lot of people didn't," I sighed, remembering how the two of us had been inseparable, best friends. *Forever.* I still remembered the first time we met, all those years ago.

"Olivia," Mommy called. I turned, skipping over to where she stood. Three strangers stood in front of her, a little boy with blond hair stared at the ground. "These are the Diamonds, and this is their son Lex." She smiled again. Daddy stood next to her, his arm wrapped around her waist. "I'm sure he'd like to see your playhouse, why don't you show him?"

"Can I?" I gaped, smiling brightly. "It's the prettiest thing in the whole wide world!"

"I bet it is!" Mrs. Diamond said, ruffling Lex's hair.

Mommy winked at Daddy. "It's just a place holder for now, until Max has time to build her a tree house."

Daddy nodded, glancing back at the Diamonds. "Yes. I had one when I was a kid, and I'll be darned if my daughter doesn't have one." I smiled up at him. "Go on, show Lex the playhouse."

I reached forward and grabbed Lex's hand, pulling him toward the backyard. He pulled against me, but I was stronger and kept going. I stopped at my playhouse, the small door open. The pink roof was littered with glitter, and it sparkled in the sunlight. I pulled him into the playhouse. A small plastic table and two matching chairs sat in the middle of the playhouse. A fake sink and oven sat to the left, plastic muffins sat on top of the oven.

"Isn't it pretty?" I beamed at my castle. Daddy often came and played with me. He would dress up and pretend to be a princess. It wasn't fun to be a princess alone.

"Yes." A grin lit up his face as well as he took in his surroundings.

I liked him. "Wanna be best friends?"

"Okay." He turned to me. "Who are you?"

"Olivia Rayne Martin!" I cheered.

He scrunched up his nose. "That's a big name."

"What's your name?"

"Lex," he said to me.

I giggled. "That's a small name."

He giggled, too. "Can we be best friends forever?"

"Of course!"

The memory faded, and I felt my sprits drop even further. I missed my best friend.

Glancing up, I saw Bethany and Ryan were talking quietly, almost like they knew I'd drifted off into the past, enjoying the memories when Lex and I were close.

"I should probably get going," Ryan said, glancing at his wrist. "I've got work in the morning, and I told my mother I would be home before too late." He stood up, and took my outstretched hand, pulling me into a standing position. "What are you girls going to do?" he moved toward the door, Bethany and I close behind him.

"Stay up late watching romantic comedies and talk about our non-existent love lives," Bethany said in a monotone voice.

"The usual," I added, feigning a chipper tone.

His lips slipped into a lopsided smile, his tongue again prodding his lip ring, twisting it slightly. "I'm sorry to miss out," he revealed. "Rain check."

"I'm holding you to that, Ryan Newly." I pointed at him once before stepping closer. His arms wrapped around me, his warm scent engulfing me in a cocoon of safety. When I stepped away, he gave Bethany a hug goodbye, too.

"Bye, Ryan," Bethany and I chimed in unison.

He waved, heading toward his car. "I'll see you ladies later." His car started and he drove off.

Bethany grabbed her backpack from her car, and we both changed into our PJ's, settling in on the couches downstairs for a movie night. It sucked that it was a school night, but it had been a long day and I didn't mind falling asleep to someone falling in love. Hopefully it would give me good dreams.

"Are you going to be okay?" Bethany murmured as the movie started.

"I will be," I answered, yawning through my words. The yawning was infectious, and soon Bethany was yawning as well. Sighing, I snuggled down into the blankets and pillow, relishing the smell of my vanilla and raspberry hair products.

My mind drifted off into La-La Land, memories of Lex and our childhood filtering into my dreams.

Chapter Ten – Late Risers

I woke up to the sound of Bethany snoring. The sun was streaming in through the windows. I stretched my arms out in front of me, feeling my muscles tense up a little.

I dropped my arms back down and yawned. The TV was on and the main menu for the movie was still going. I reached forwards and grabbed the remote, turning the TV off. I rubbed my eyes wearily and got up off the couch.

In the morning, I tended to be clumsy, and it remained that way today as well. I tripped over the rug and hit the ground. I felt the urge to curse, but held in the evil words. My fall was loud, and therefore woke up Bethany.

"You're loud," she mumbled sleepily.

"Shut up," I grumbled, rubbing my knees before I stood back up. I walked into the bathroom and looked at my reflection. It was blurry. I grabbed blindly at the counter, putting on my glasses. "Ew," I winced. With a little water, I washed off the excess makeup and smoothed down my hair again.

When I walked back into living room, Bethany was still zonked out on the couch. I laughed slightly and searched for my phone. No doubt it was hiding somewhere between the cushions, it liked to do that. *A lot.*

Finally, my fingers connected with the plastic case of my phone, and I pulled it out to check the time. When the screen opened up, I nearly dropped my phone back onto the couch.

Today was a school day, it was almost ten o'clock. *Sugar honey iced tea*!

"Bethany Bridges!" I practically screamed at her.

She jolted, nearly landing on the floor. "What?" Clearly, she was in no mood to be so rudely awakened.

"It's Wednesday!" I shrieked. She tried to think of why Wednesday was important. "You are so dense sometimes, Bethany! School!" I said the word loudly to add emphasis.

Her eyes widened. "Oh crap." She shot off the couch and we both scrambled to get ready for school.

I'd never managed to get ready so fast before. Within ten minutes, I was dressed, primped, and fed. Bethany, likewise, had sped through her morning rituals and was ready to go. We got in the car, and she started toward school.

"We're so going to get busted for being late," I groaned. "My mom's going to have a cow!"

"Yeah? Well then my mom is going to have a cruise ship!" Bethany replied, watching the speedometer.

I blinked. "That sounds painful."

"It will be. Now stop talking, I need to focus on speeding!" She groaned.

"If we get there at the perfect moment, we'll be there right before classes get out, and we won't have to go to the office for being late," I tried to think positively.

"I hope we get there at the right time then," she mumbled, her eyes glued to the road, and her foot pressing farther down on the gas pedal.

Like I'd predicted, it was a few minutes before second period class let out, and we could easily slip into the crowd unnoticed once they got out of their classes.

"I need to get my stuff out of my locker. I'll see you in homeroom." Bethany waved, heading down the hallway toward her locker. I nodded, moving in the opposite direction to find my locker and grab my homework.

One of the main doors opened and blinding light streamed in. A shadow splayed across the ground before the door shut, the shadow disappearing. I looked up, expecting a teacher back from a cigarette break.

Instead, Lex came in. Droplets fell from his blond hair onto the white material of his shirt. He stopped dead in his tracks when he saw me. "Hey…"

I raised an eyebrow confused. "You still have them?" His hand went up to the red glasses on his face. "I thought you threw them away."

"I tried," he acknowledged. "Mom took them before I could, claiming I would need them again one day. Guess she was right."

I smirked, touching my own glasses. "Guess so. I'm sort of jealous though, I miss my red ones."

He grimaced. "I'm sorry about that."

"So you admit it was your fault?" I challenged, raising an eyebrow. I'd always known he did it on purpose, even if he claimed otherwise.

"Suppose I should own up to it at some point," he muttered.

"You have denied it for a while," I agreed, grinning. A glance at the clock told me we still had a few minutes before the rest of the student body was released from class.

He rolled his eyes at me. "Whatever, just take the apology and move on."

"Apology accepted. Now, why *are* you wearing the nerdy red glasses?"

"My normal alarm clock was missing this morning," he replied.

I cocked an eyebrow at him. "What are you talking about?"

He grinned slyly. That wasn't a good sign. "The morning dance routine of course."

I felt the blood drain from my face. "Excuse me?" the words were barely audible. There was no way he knew about my morning ritual.

"Don't kid, Honeybee, you know what I'm talking about. Every morning around six o'clock, you blast your music really loud and have a dance party. They're quite loud, but very entertaining." He winked.

"Who else have you told?" The realization that he could've told other people about it made me sick to my stomach. The possibilities were endless, people halfway across the world could know about my morning dancing. I wanted to find a rock and hide under it.

"Well, no one yet. Why? Did you want a bigger audience next time?" I felt my cheeks heat up. Why did I love him? *How* could I love him? "That could be arranged," he sneered.

"I hate you." I glared at him, crossing my arms over my chest.

"You asked why I'm wearing glasses. I'm simply answering your question."

"You bug me," I grumbled, pulling my bag higher on my back.

"Honestly, stop saying things that relate to honeybees. Now, if you don't mind, I need to get to my locker."

"Why? To get your books?"

He scoffed. "I need to get my contacts. I'm not wearing the siren glasses all day long," he said, moving around me. "Until homeroom, Honeybee."

"Yippee," I deadpanned, continuing down the hall. The bell rang and the sound of footsteps and doors opening filled the hallway.

"Oh, Honeybee." I turned back to him. He was smirking again. That had to be a bad sign.

"What?"

"I'm so coming over to your next dance party." He winked, walking away.

"Who said you were invited?" I mumbled to myself, losing myself in the crowd.

The rest of the day went by in a blur, every class blended into one big fog. I was thankful when school was over. I walked down the path, past the tall trees that cast their shadows down on me. I tilted my head to glance at the sky before I continued walking.

The bench where I normally sat was vacant, so I slipped down onto it. Bethany would be along soon enough.

I watched the car drive past me down the street, absently playing with my hair as I did so. I sat cross legged on the bench, and pulled out my iPod, sticking one earbud in. I started humming along with the song.

"Boo!" A voice said right by my ear.

I jumped, my feet slamming to the ground. I turned to glare, my gaze faltering upon seeing who it was. "Jeremiah?" I raised an eyebrow. "What do you want?"

"Bethany," he murmured dreamily, a lazy smile on his face.

I rolled my eyes. "Does it look like I have her?"

He shook his head. "No, it doesn't. I was just telling you what I wanted."

I turned away from him, already annoyed by his presence. My heart ached for Bethany who had been dealing with him for the past few weeks. "Was there something in particular that you needed help with?"

He sank into the spot next to me, his arm draped over the edge of the bench. "No. I'm just waiting for, Bethany."

"You guys are in the same class, why are you waiting?"

"She said she needed a few minutes to get ready," he shrugged, stifling a yawn.

"Where is she going?" I groaned. Couldn't he give me a straight answer? Why did men beat around the bush? Why did anyone?

"Ask her." He jerked his thumb behind us. I turned and saw Bethany walking over. Her white skinny jeans and pale blue blouse made her skin seem even tanner. Her makeup looked like she'd touched it up, and her hair had more work done to it than earlier.

"Bethany, where are you going all dolled up?" I asked. Jeremiah once again grinned.

She glanced at Jeremiah, her lips in a firm line. "Jeremiah, can we have a minute?"

"Sure, I'll go get my car." He hopped off the bench and started toward the parking lot. Bethany's eyes followed him, her lips pursed in thought.

I raised an eyebrow. "You going to tell me what's going on?"

She sighed, pushing her hair out of her face. "I think he slipped me something. I don't know why, but I agreed to go out on a date with him." I gaped. "I know," she mumbled, pulling on the ends of her hair lightly. "I'm hoping, after this date, he'll see I'm really not the girl he wants, and just go away."

"You're going on a date with him to get out of dealing with him in the future?"

"See!" She smiled. "You understand me." I smirked, shaking my head as Jeremiah's car pulled up to the curb. Our eyes moved to him.

"You ready?" he questioned, revving the engine impatiently.

"I'm taking my own car," she shot back, crossing her arms over her chest. "I'll meet you at the restaurant."

He sighed, and nodded. "Fine. But don't stand me up," he warned. She nodded, waving him on.

"Are you going to stand him up?" I giggled, knowing it was something she would do.

"No," she muttered begrudgingly. "I want to get this over with. I plan to be done before six tonight."

"Yeah? Home early because of homework or a stomach ache?" I grinned, giving out the usual excuses I'd heard on T.V. I learned everything I knew about love from movies and T.V. shows.

"More like I'm just going home," she replied easily. "I'm not going to con my way out of a date. That will just leave room for him to assume I wanted to go longer, when really, I had no interest at all."

I gasped, feigning shock. "You're so much smarter than any of my love advisers."

"I know." She glanced at her watch. "I should go. I still have to call my mom and tell her what's going on."

"Have fun with that," I laughed.

"Do you want a ride home?" she asked, a smile lighting her eyes at the excuse to be even later to her date.

"No, you go. Have fun, flirt and stuff," I said, raising a fist in excitement. "I'll walk home." It wasn't that far. Plus, I ate too much junk food. A walk would be good for me.

"Fine," she grumbled, pulling her keys out of her purse. "Call me when you get home so I know you didn't get murdered or kidnapped."

"What if I sprain my ankle?" No one ever cared about ordinary, everyday things that caused people to not get home.

"If you sprain your ankle, call my mom. She'd love to practice some of her first aid on you, I'm sure," she laughed. She pulled me in for a quick hug before heading toward her car. "See you later!"

"Bye," I called, before turning and walking home. My Bethany was growing up. Soon enough, she'd be flirting with boys she actually liked, staying out until obscene hours of the night, and gallivanting around the town with her boy toy.

Smirking, I slipped my headphones in and turned the music up. It was a beautiful day for a walk.

Chapter Eleven – To Curse, or Not to Curse

As I was stepping up to the house, my phone started vibrating in my purse. I dug it out and flipped it open. "Hello?" I mumbled, searching for my house keys so I could get out of the heat. I swear it had climbed ten degrees on the way home. I felt gross and sweaty.

"Hey, honey," Mom greeted.

"Hey, Mom, what's up?" My fingers clasped around my keys. Hurriedly, I unlocked the door and stepped inside. The air was considerably colder, and I shivered at the temperature change.

"I'm not coming home for dinner tonight. I have to work late. There is some money on my dresser for you to order pizza. You can have your friends over if you'd like, but I'm already exhausted, so no late nighters," she sighed. I could imagine her leaning against her desk, chin in her hand, as she talked to me. No doubt, a cold cup of coffee sat on her desk untouched. She always kept busy at work.

"Alright. I hope you finish up soon." I let my purse fall to the floor and slipped off my shoes. The wood flooring was chilly on my bare feet.
"Thanks, honey. I'll talk to you later, clean up after yourself," she requested.

"I will. Bye." I clicked the conversation to an end and set my phone down on the small table near the door where Mom dropped mail, keys, and whatever else she had on her person when she came in the door after work.

Walking upstairs, I yawned. My body hadn't woken up all day. All I wanted to do was fall into bed and take a nap. The top stair took me by surprise, and I nearly tripped. I hated being tired. I always forgot the simplest of things, like the fact there was another step.

Once in my room, I shut my door and moved to my dresser, pulling out a pair of black cotton pajama shorts and a dark purple tank top, laying both articles of clothing on top of my dresser.

I turned on my iPod, letting music blare through the speakers. I pulled off the lacey white dress that hugged my curves, laying it over the chair. Next went the leggings. My muscles relaxed, swaying with the music. I pulled on cotton shorts, still dancing around to the music. Anywhere else, I wouldn't dare dance around in shorts and a bra, but in my room, I didn't see the problem.

As I turned to grab my tank top, a curse word nearly spilled from my lips. Twice in one day was not a good sign. I clutched the tank top across my exposed abdomen and bra, closing my eyes. The heat rose to my cheeks, and I wished I had thought to shut the curtains before dancing around.

Across the street, Lex stood in his window watching me with an amused smirk. Considering how big the smirk was, he'd been watching me for a few minutes. He gave a small wave, still watching me.

Angrily, I shut the curtains and fell down on the bed groaning. "Curse that boy." My phone rang, without looking I picked it up and placed it to my ear. "What?"

"You ruin all my fun," was the reply before the call abruptly ended.

It took a few moments for realization to hit me. "Lex!" I growled. After pulling my tank top on, I searched for my flip flops, heading in Lex's direction.

When I reached his front door, I noticed that his parents weren't home yet. I supposed they were still at work or something. The door was unlocked so I went straight inside. Lex never was one for details and things like locking the door or minding his own business when his next door neighbor forgot to close her curtains.

I stepped inside and shivered at the cold temperature they kept their house in. I slipped off my shoes and raced up the stairs going straight to Lex's room. I pushed open the door and was met by, as he would call it, a *manly* scream. I froze in the doorway.

"Honeybee! What the heck are you doing?" Lex danced around shirtless, hurrying to pull his shorts on. I could've sworn he was dressed when he decided to be a peeping tom.

"Knockings for losers?" I quoted, unsure of myself.

"Stop looking," he demanded.

I frowned and put my hands on my hips. "Funny, you were looking at me," I recalled, angrily.

"That's different, I'm a guy."

"That's no excuse," I retorted.

"Get out!" He groaned, zipping his shorts. I stuck my tongue out and spun on my heel, leaving his room and shutting the door. I skipped down the stairs, grabbed my shoes, and made my way back across the street.

I slammed my door shut and walked into the kitchen. My hands closed around a tall glass of water and then nearly dropped it when the door opened and slammed again, shaking the glasses in the cupboard. Setting down the water, I ventured back into the entry way, preparing to sprint back to the kitchen and grab a knife if needed.

Lex stood there, fully clothed now, in gray shorts and a white t-shirt. His arms were crossed over his chest. I mirrored his pose. "What?"

"You know what, you peeping tom," he accused, the trace of a sneer on his lips. "I should call the cops."

"Somehow, I think the police would side with me when I told them the full story." I assured him. "Besides, I didn't know you weren't dressed."

"You didn't bother knocking to find out either, did you?"

"You wouldn't have," I countered, holding my glare. It probably wasn't as intimidating as I'd hoped. He rolled his eyes and walked into the living room barefoot. I supposed he'd already kicked his shoes off. He was way too comfortable in my house. "What are you doing?"

"Whatever I want," he replied, sinking into my couch.

"You're not planning on staying are you?" I raised an eyebrow cautiously. He reached for the remote and turned on the TV, answering my question. I groaned and ran back upstairs.

"Order food," he called absently.

Curse that boy.

I paced back and forth in my room, wondering what to do about Lex. I couldn't call Bethany, she was on a date. She would probably welcome the excuse to leave, but part of me was convinced she was actually enjoying the attention. Sighing, I shook my head. I wouldn't call her. Even *if* Lex was taking my living room captive.

After a little while, I made my way back downstairs. Lex was still lounging on my couch, looking more than comfortable. I swept my hair over my shoulder and glared at him through my glasses. "You know, I didn't say you could stay."

"Didn't I say to order food?" He didn't even look away from the T.V.

"Why are you here?" I leaned against the frame of the archway that led into the living room. "Doesn't your mother cook for you anymore?"

"Yeah, but my parents are out."

"And you expect me to feed you?" I hissed.

"Yeah," he yawned. He stretched out on the couch, the hem of his shirt riding up, offering me a quick glimpse of his abs before he covered them back up. "Unless your mom's here, then she can feed both of us."

"She won't be home till later."

"Then I guess the duty to feed me falls to you, Honeybee. Get to work." He beamed, a devilish spark in his forest green gaze.

I glared at him and turned towards the kitchen. I picked the phone up off of the counter and dialed a pizza place. "What kind do you want?" I yelled, not explaining my meaning. He would understand.

"Cheese," he shouted.

I rolled my eyes at his simplicity when it came to pizza. I for one liked to try new things. Oreos, crushed up Doritos, sprinkles; anything weird. Lex used to try new combinations with me, hence *used to*. After I ordered the pizzas, I walked back into the living room.

Lex was still sitting on the couch. "Did you order food?"

"Yes," I said. I stood in front of him and stared at the TV. "What are you watching?"

"I think there's a Disney movie coming on soon. Sit down," he instructed.

I shook my head. "No way, I'm sitting over there." I pointed towards the seat opposite him.

"I demand you sit down here." He told me, slapping the spot next to him.

"Can't make me," I teased.

He grabbed the back of my tank top, tugging me into the spot beside him "Yes I can." He smiled, still holding onto my top. I assumed it was so that I couldn't leave.

"If I wasn't protecting your dignity from the truth, I would show you how strong I am and walk away without any trouble," I told him.

He scoffed. "You'll never be stronger than I am."

"I was when we were younger," I reminded him.

"I let you win because you're a girl," he assured me, his arm moving to rest around my hips.

"Funny, but that excuse won't fly with me." I pushed his arm away.

"It's not an excuse," he feigned disgust, putting his arm around me again.

I grabbed his arm and let it fall back in his own lap. But, being the egotistical guy that he was, Lex couldn't lose. His arm dropped my shoulders, curling my hair around his fingers. If he wasn't dating Cassy, the moment would've been a cute couple's faux-fight.

"Lex," I grumbled. Sighing, he took his arm off of me.

The TV in front of us glared a bright blue and animated ocean. The words *"Finding Nemo"* floated across the screen.

Lex gasped. "Isn't this your favorite movie in the whole wide world?"

My mouth dropped open. "How did you know that?"

He glanced over at me, a glint in his eyes. "You told me, when we were like ... eight or nine."

"You remembered that?"

"Course I did. What are best friends for?" I was at a loss for words. "You don't remember that kind of stuff about me?" he asked quietly. There was something in his gaze. It almost looked like he was hurt.

"I remember that you love Tinker Bell." He smiled. "And that you got mad at me for dressing up like her for Halloween."

"You knew she was off limits." He winked.

"You mocked, Peter. You knew *he* was off limits," I retorted, crossing my arms over my chest.

"Don't bring up, Peter Pansy. He doesn't compare with Tink." It always amused me how serious he was about his dislike for Peter Pan.

"He does in my book." I settled back against the cushions, aware of how close our bodies were on the couch. If he moved even slightly, we would be touching. Heat spread across my face.

"Where is your book? I need to burn it. Peter Pan is a fairy boy. You know he wore a skirt, right?" he double checked.

"I recall a certain video game character that wore a green skirt as well. I think you called it a tunic though," I hinted.

His eyes widened. "Don't ever compare Peter Pansy the fairy boy and Link the hero. Ever. They're nothing alike."

I giggled and turned my eyes back to the movie. It was about the point where Nemo's mom went to save the eggs, and the evil fish killed her. A hand shot in front of my eyes and I couldn't help but smile.

"Don't watch this part. It's too scary for you."

"Thank you, Lex."

"That's the first time you've said thank you to me in like ... a long time."

"And who do we blame for that?" I remarked sarcastically.

"Bethany," he answered quickly. I hit his arm. "Ow." He rubbed it a moment.

"Just be quiet and let me watch my favorite movie in peace." I pulled my legs up so I was sitting cross legged. He complied and shut his mouth.

About ten minutes later the doorbell rang.

"Nose goes!" I cried loudly, putting my finger on my nose.

Lex gaped at me. "What? I didn't know we still did that!"

I stuck my tongue out at him. "Sucker! Now go pay for the pizza." He sighed and stood up, heading towards the door. "Put it in the kitchen," I added.

As Dory and Marlin raced around trying to find Nemo, I heard Lex in the background pay and shut the door. He walked into the kitchen, set the food down, and came back in.

I went past him into the kitchen, opening the cupboard door to search for strange foods to put on the pizza. I grabbed the Oreos, Lays chips, and crushed them up all over the pizza. I cut up the pizza, grabbed some sodas from the fridge, and took it all back into the living room. I set it on the table and watched as Lex stared at it for a few moments.

"I said cheese pizza," he finally spoke. "What is this?"

"Yes, I know you did. But, this is like having the entrée, side dish, and desert all at the same time," I insisted, sitting back down.

He put his hand on my knee, sending shivers up and down my spine. "If I faint or something, please promise you'll call an ambulance. I don't want to die from this," he muttered gravely.

I laughed and placed my hand on top of his. "Don't worry. If you faint, I'll call for help."

I watched as he slowly picked up a piece of pizza and moved it towards his now open mouth. He stuck his tongue towards the pizza and licked it. I giggled. He glanced at me a moment. "Don't mock,"

"Chicken," I taunted, raising an eyebrow.

"Am not," he declared. The pizza was still in front of his mouth. As if to prove his point, he took a deep breath and stuck almost half of the piece of pizza in his mouth. I heard the crunching as he chewed on Oreo crumbles. He scrunched up his face and continued eating. After a few seconds, and a few more incomprehensible facial expressions, he swallowed.

As I waited for him to compliment my ability to create great pizza, I turned back to the movie. Dory and Marlin were racing around, trying to avoid bombs and get away from Bruce.

A light thud made me turn around. I raised an eyebrow. Lex lay on the couch, eyes closed.

"Lex?"

He was probably acting like he'd fainted to mess with me. I poked him a few times, watching for a reaction, but there was nothing. A thought struck me. What if that sickness, that was causing him to be somewhat nice at times, had killed him?

Oh dear.

"Lex, seriously."

He was still breathing, that was a good sign. I stood up and moved in front of him, peering down at him. I almost poked him again when I remembered how people poked dead things, and he couldn't be dead.

The minute the idea of death popped into my head, I started to worry. What if he was allergic to something in the pizza, or Oreos, or Lays? I gulped. What if I had accidentally poisoned Lex?

My heart almost stopped when his chest did. He wasn't breathing. Panic swept through my body at an alarming pace. My heartbeat quickened. I searched my brain for something. First Aid! Of course, I'd taken one of those classes for some career education program in school. I couldn't believe what I was about to do. Telling myself this was to save him; I leaned down and opened his mouth, hesitating the whole time.

Our lips touched, and as I should have predicted all along, he was fine. So fine in fact, that he decided to return the mouth to mouth gesture. Taken by surprise, I didn't know how to react. My instincts kicked in, and my eyes closed as I was lost in the kiss. He leaned up against my lips, deepening the kiss. He placed his hand against my cheek.

A small voice in the back of my head was screaming at me, telling me to stop what I was doing. I knew it was stupid, letting myself get wrapped up in him again, but logic couldn't seem to reason with the feelings inside my heart, cheering at his touch.

The movie in the background reached the part where the bombs went off. The loud explosions made me jolt, ending the kiss. Our breath mingled together, my eyes remaining shut. I felt his thumb touch my lips gently.

I took the chance and opened my eyes. He was laying there, a small smile on his lips, and his eyes were still closed. I bit my lip and smiled. He looked content about kissing me. Lex Diamond was content with kissing me. *Honeybee*.

A yell from Dory and Marlin being chased by that evil glow fish startled him, and he opened his eyes. He caught me staring.

He smiled at me a moment before he sat up. "Thanks for saving me. I knew I could count on you." He winked, leaning back against the couch. I leaned back, and this time I let him put his arm around me.

Chapter Twelve – Too Complicated for Curses

Lex was lying on the couch next to me, another piece of pizza in his hands. "I miss your pizza concoctions." He took another bite.

"Good." I grabbed my Pepsi off the table and took a sip. He stuck his hand out for it. I slowly relinquished my soda to him. He took a long swig of it, before handing it back to me. I shook it around slightly; empty. I frowned. "Jerk."

"Baby."

"Prat."

He laughed, his head lolling back. "Wow. That's a little harsh," he told me.

I shrugged. "You did pretend you were dying just so that I would feel obligated to save you." I knew it was bad I reacted so calmly to him kissing me. I should've been outraged that he had the audacity to kiss me when I was trying to save his life. But instead, it was like I was on a sugar rush. My heart was beating erratically, and my thoughts were moving way to fast to figure out what they were all for.

"I like kissing you, you're good at it," Lex murmured, covering a yawn.

"Thanks," I stammered, a blush coloring my face.

He smirked and ran his fingers along my cheek. "You're welcome, Honeybee." He dropped his hand back down to the couch and slipped his fingers in between mine.

The simple gesture made my emotions run wild as it brought back memories of the first time he held my hand, the first time he kissed me. Right before he walked away.

My breathing turned ragged as I struggled to keep my emotions in check, reliving all of the times he'd hurt me. All the times he'd walked away, all the times he'd watched me fall. How many times was it going to take before I got it in my head? Lex was bad news.

"Honeybee, are you okay?" he shifted closer to me. I nodded, refusing to answer. "I don't buy it. You can tell me," he murmured.

"What are we doing, Lex?" I bit my lip, hoping my eyes didn't spill any tears.

"What do you mean?"

"It's like some sick cycle we keep repeating," I muttered, looking away from the T.V. screen. "You act sweet, something romantic happens, and then you walk away." *And you leave me to pick up the pieces of my broken heart.* I wiped a tear from my eye.

"Honeybee, are you crying?" There was concern at the edge of his words. He reached over wiping away the tears that slipped down my cheeks. He brushed the hair from my eyes and placed his forehead against mine. "What's wrong?"

"You were my best friend in the whole world. But now, I don't even know what we are." I bit my lip, cursing my emotions for giving in so easily. "I'm tired of being hurt."

"I'm not going to hurt you," he whispered, his breath hot on my skin.

"You already have, so many times." I moved away from him, looking down. "I think you should leave, Lex."

The silence between us made me feel numb. Even the sounds of the T.V seemed to fade into the background. The only thing I could hear was our breath brushing by each other as we exhaled.

His lips set in a firm line. "Fine." His voice was cold, making me want to shrink away.

I was vaguely aware of the door slamming shut, and the sound of sobs coming from my own throat. My heart ached for the boy it would never have, the love that would never be reciprocated.

Taking a deep breath, I shook myself. I needed something to get my mind off of Lex. I was so sick of crying over him. At least if I watched a movie I could pretend that's what I was crying about. I searched through the movies, and ended up with Sleepless in Seattle.

After grabbing chocolate ice cream from the freezer and a spoon, I moved back into the living room and sunk down onto the couch. It was time to remind myself that not all love stories ended in heartbreak.

Forty-five minutes later, tears were on my face over the fact Meg Ryan and Tom Hanks weren't together. They were perfect for each other, yet they weren't together. It was depressing. Even though I knew the ending was happy, I couldn't help the tears.

The doorbell ringing nearly gave me a heart attack, the ice cream tub slipping from my fingers into my lap. I quickly set it on the coffee table and tossed off the blanket.

I shivered in the cool house, mentally reminding myself to grab a sweater before returning to the movie.

I pulled open the door and gasped slightly. His head looked up, lip ring glinting in the light coming from the porch light. I didn't understand. "Ryan, what are you doing here?"

He'd texted me a while ago, just to say hey. I'd text back a few times before telling him I wasn't feeling good and needed to lie down. I wasn't sick, just emotionally drained.

He enveloped me in a hug. A good hug always made things better, and Ryan gave good hugs. "Can I come in?" he asked when he pulled back. He lifted a brown paper bag. "I brought soup just in case you needed it." He was too sweet.

A small smile flickered across my features, and I nodded. We went back into the living room. He didn't even complain when he saw what movie I was watching. The cup of soup warmed my body. Maybe ice cream wasn't the only thing that could help a broken heart. Chicken noodle soup helped, too.

My big moment of emotions was the end of the movie when Meg Ryan and Tom Hanks finally got together. Ryan pretended to be all sappy about the end, which made me laugh. He even went so far as to wipe away imaginary tears.

When the credits started to roll, I got up and went to grab another movie.

"Something masculine," Ryan pleaded, stretching out on the couch. I pulled out one of the Bond movies. He nodded his approval and I moved back to the couch, picking up the ice cream container. It was almost all gone.

Ryan shivered. "Your feet are cold." I raised an eyebrow. How did he even know my feet were cold? "I can feel your feet on my legs," he murmured knowingly.

"Don't judge my body temperature," I chided, dipping my spoon into the ice cream.

"I wasn't," he gasped.

"Sure," I mumbled, shoveling more chocolate in my mouth. He dipped his spoon into the container and shared the ice cream with me.

Halfway through the movie, the front door opened.

I turned, straining my neck to see who it was. Mom walked in the house, her purse draped over her arm and her hair in a tight bun. She was wearing one of her pencil skirts and a white blouse. She spotted me and Ryan sitting on the couch together and raised her eyebrows

"Hello, Ryan," she welcomed, shooting a wary glance at me.

Ryan turned and smiled at her. "Hey, Mrs. Martin."

"Call me Debby." She waved away the formality. "I didn't know you were coming over tonight," she noted, walking into the living room.

"It was kind of impromptu," he replied, watching the movie out of the corner of his eye.

"I see." She smiled.

"How was work?" I asked.

"Oh you know, lots of fun," she quipped. "I'm sorry I got home so late, did you eat already?" she started toward the kitchen.

"Yeah," I called back to her. "Pizza."

"I hope you didn't feed that friend of yours the pizza you and Lex used to make," she said. The ingredients were still out in the kitchen, which probably tipped her off to what kind of pizza we had.

My chest ached. "I didn't." Ryan nudged my shoulder, giving me a smile. "Are you a mind reader?" I laughed.

"Not exactly," he said coyly. "Just perceptive."

"It's a wonder you don't already have a girlfriend," I mused.

"I haven't found the right girl yet." He shrugged.

"Or she hasn't realized you like her yet," I sighed. A flash of emotion passed over his face, almost like he was afraid. Realization hit me. "That's totally it, isn't it? She doesn't know?" he frowned, looking away. I grinned. "Awh, that's adorable! Want to talk about it?"

He shook his head quickly. "No, I don't."

"Come on, I'll tell you all about ... *him,* and you tell me all about *her.* It'll be fun. We can even go into my room so my mother doesn't hear," I prodded him, a smile on my face.

"Are you going to bug me about it until I say yes?" his deadpanned.

"Yes, probably," I confirmed with a nod.

He sighed, pressing pause on the movie. "Fantastic." Laughing, I stood and pulled him to his feet. A blanket was wrapped around my shoulders. We walked upstairs to my room. I shut the door *and* the curtains. "Isn't this the kind of thing that makes parents worry?" he asked, smirking.

"Oh shut up. Mom knows I wouldn't do that." But sure enough, a few seconds later there was a knock on my door.

"Honey, I'd prefer if you left the door opened." Mom glanced at Ryan warily.

"We're just going to talk, and if it goes anything past that, you have full permission to send me to some boarding school where I'll waste away and become a nun or something."

She cocked an eyebrow. "That's what they all say. Keep the door open. I might spontaneously burst in the room. Just remember that," she threatened before she left.

I closed the door, leaving it open just a crack. I sat down on my bed, wrapping the covers around me. "Sit," I instructed, pointing to the bed.

"What if your mom walks in?" he asked, sitting down on the bed cross legged.

"She won't. Now, tell me about your crush," I giggled, pulling my blankets around myself.

He tossed one of my stuffed animals at me. "Why don't you go first? Tell me about your major crush on, Lex. Tell me about when you two were younger. What led you to falling in love with him?" I glanced down at the blue penguin in my hands. He raised an eyebrow expectantly.

I shrugged. "It just kind of happened. We spent all our time together, told each other everything, literally. Our favorite colors, movies, and our thoughts on political things at school. We even gossiped about who was dating who." He laughed. "The crush just developed over time, and I was convinced he loved me as well. I obviously watched far too many sappy love stories then, also," I muttered.

"Have you ever told him how you feel?" he asked. I shook my head. "You know guys can't read minds, right?" he smiled.

"And all this time I thought he knew how I felt!" I exclaimed.

"Sorry, someone was supposed to tell you, I believe mothers usually deliver the delicate news," he explained.

I groaned and fell back into my pillows. "Why couldn't she have told me this earlier? It would've made life so much easier."

"Doubtful," he argued.

"Boys are just so gosh darn confusing!" I grumbled.

"F.Y.I., girls are just as confusing."

"Doubtful," I mimicked. "We girls are very good at showing our feelings."

He rolled his eyes at my comment. "As a guy who has dealt with girls in the past, I know your gender is nothing less than confusing."

"Oh, and how many experiences have you had dealing with confusing girls?" I asked, smirking.

"Enough," he replied, shooting me a wink.

"Men. I never get a straight answer from your species." I glared at the bedspread.

"We're good at avoiding things like that," he agreed, grinning.

"Apparently," I replied.

"I have a question for you," he murmured, leaning his elbows on his knees.

"Shoot."

"How exactly did you get your nickname?" he wondered, a small smile glinting his lips. "I've been curious about it since I first heard it."

The memory of how I got my silly nickname presented itself in my mind, and my lips started moving. "Well, it happened about ten years ago," I started. "I was sitting in my front lawn picking flowers." It was like I was transported back in time, back to that moment. I could feel the soft grass beneath me, and smell the flowers scattered around me. "Lex just got back from riding his bike with his dad when he came over to my house." The pink helmet, borrowed from his mother, trailed behind him. Bike rides with his father were a regular occurrence back then. "We were just talking about playing in the tree house when all of sudden I started screaming bloody murder," I told him, shaking my head at the memory. Lex had dropped the helmet and stared at me in horror, like I had grown a second head. "Mom came bursting out of the door, a kitchen knife in her hand. Dad even came a little faster than normal."

The look of panic in Dad's eyes when he came out to see what was wrong still haunted me sometimes. I would have nightmares where that look of panic filled his eyes right before the car slammed into him. I bit my lip to keep my emotions in check.

"So as it turned out, I'd grabbed hold of a flower with a honeybee on it. Now, if you knew Lex better, you would know he is lazy. Even when he was younger. For some reason, he used to call me by my full name. When I got stung, and over reacted because I was a kid, he took the opportunity to change my name. He's called me Honeybee ever since." *I'm always going to call you Honeybee.* The promise of an eight year old lasted much longer than I expected.

"It's too bad he's still not an eight-year-old. I think I would've liked him better when he was younger," Ryan mused.

I smirked. "Most would," I agreed. "Now! I demand that you tell me about your crush." I couldn't help the glee that fled to my face.

"There's really not much to tell."
"There's always something to tell," I replied. "Now spill it before I smack you."

He laughed. "Gee, Olivia, you're threatening me now?"

"Yeah. So spill." I said. He groaned. "Just tell me a little about her, what's she like?"

"Fine," he caved. "She's got a great personality. She's funny, smart, easily embarrassed, kind of sarcastic, and all around sweet."

"What was the first thing you noticed about her?" I asked, wanting to know all the details of his crush.

"Well, she's short," he laughed.

"After that?"

"She's got pretty eyes,"

"Next?"

"She's not afraid to be herself, even if that means making people feel awkward." He laughed.

"So what stopped you from asking her out?" I asked.

He sighed, leaning against his knees. "She just doesn't seem interested, so I'm being careful. I don't want to get her heart involved before we know what's going to happen between us." I knew I liked Ryan for good reason. "Is that enough–"

I jumped when the door burst open, swinging back and slamming into the wall. "Mom!" I yelled.

She had a funny look on her face and was standing in a ninja like pose in the doorway. "Just making sure nothing fishy was going on." She said, grabbing the door and leaving.

I clutched my chest, my heart still pounding. "Sorry about her. I never knew she acted like this when I had guys in the house. She never acted like this when Lex was around."

"It's okay. I bet if I brought you over and took you upstairs; within five minutes my mom would have an excuse to come check in on us."

"What is it with mothers and bursting in like that?" I laughed, leaning into my pillows.

"It makes them feel powerful I guess," he laughed along. "So, did you ask all that you wanted to ask?" He questioned. I wanted to ask him what her name was, but since he wasn't forthcoming, I wouldn't force it from him. I nodded and we went back downstairs.

We finished watching the movie around ten, I felt bad keeping Ryan so long, but it was nice to have someone there. Mom had gone up to her room around nine. She made sure to give both of us threatening glares, warning us not to do anything while unsupervised.

I flipped the TV off, and turned to Ryan.

He stretched his arms forwards a moment before dropping them and sighing. He glanced over at me. "I think it's about time I got going," he said.

"Probably. Do you have to work tomorrow?" I asked.

"Yeah, I'm opening tomorrow," he replied.

I gasped, my cheeks heating up in embarrassment. "Ryan, I'm sorry! I shouldn't have kept you so long,"

"Don't worry about it, Livie. You needed someone and I was perfectly happy to be that someone for you," he said.

"Thank you, Ryan. I don't deserve to have such good friends, all I do is complain to them about Lex," I mumbled, crossing my arms over my chest.

"If it gets to be too much, I'll just go beat him up so he won't be able to mess with you for a while." He stood up, pulling me to my feet. I walked outside to his car with him.

"Thanks for walking me to my car." A cute grin lingered on his face.

"You're welcome." I smiled. "I hope you get some sleep, sorry for keeping you out so long."

"It was fun," he promised. Silence dragged on between us. I bit my lip, trying to think of what to say. "So, um," he started, almost like he felt uncomfortable. "What would you say if I asked you out for coffee sometime?"

"What do you mean?" butterflies erupted in my stomach.

"Just to get to know each other better, as friends," he offered.

I couldn't help the grin that spread across my face. "Are you asking me on a date?"

"A mostly platonic one." He nodded. "Just to get our minds off these other people. Who knows, maybe something great will happen from it," he thought.

"Okay,"

"Okay what?" he pressed, playing with his lip ring.

My eyes lingered on the ring a moment before I remembered to answer. I'd never really thought of lip rings as attractive, but they definitely were. "We can go on a mostly platonic coffee date," I told him.

"Really?" he smiled.

"Yes, really," I giggled, feeling bubbly.

"How about this Friday?" he leaned against his car, flipping his keys around his fingers.

A breeze drifted by, rustling the leaves on the tree. I shivered, rubbing my arms. "Five?"

He nodded quickly, smiling back at me. "It's a date."

"Sounds perfect," I spoke softly, biting my lip. "It's time you got home though." I stepped into his arms, delighting in the warmth he offered.

"Your mom is watching us from her room," he murmured into my ear softly.

I burst out laughing, hugging him tighter before letting go. "Mothers."

"Really," he laughed. He got into his car, putting the keys in the ignition. "See you Friday, Olivia."

"Until then," I murmured wistfully.

He waved goodbye and backed out of my driveway, driving off towards his house. I stood out there a few more minutes, watching his car lights disappear into the darkness. I grinned to myself before going back inside. I was going to have my first date.

Chapter Thirteen – Fighting for First

My tray slapped down loudly on to the gray plastic table top, and I slumped into the chair.

Bethany looked up, raising an eyebrow at my rough entrance. "You alright?"

I smiled. "Yeah, sorry. How was your date?" We hadn't had the time to talk about it yet, and I was incredibly curious. I almost hoped it went well and they were in love, just because it would give her something to gush about and blush over.

The drop in her features told me it hadn't gone well. "Jeremiah and I are so not compatible." She ran her hands through her ebony hair. "All he talked about was football, and how awesome he is. He couldn't say enough about it." She laughed. "It was literally an hour and a half of him promoting himself to me, like I would fall for his charm."

"Or lack thereof," I added. She snorted, covering her mouth with her hands. I grinned before glancing at the body headed our way. The smile fell from my face. "Careful, Prince Charming is headed this way."

She frowned and turned around as Jeremiah sauntered over. He lifted the sunglasses from his eyes, grinning at Bethany. "Hey." He slid into the spot next to her, close enough that their arms brushed.

She grimaced, moving away from him. "Hi."

"That was fun last night, right?" he winked, nudging her arm.

She shot an exasperated look my way. "Listen, Jeremiah," she started, frowning as he closed the distance between them.

"Yes, Buttercup?" he cooed, leaning his face closer to hers.

"I thought I made it pretty clear last night that a second date isn't going to happen," Bethany stated, pushing against his chest to stop him coming any closer.

His hands closed over hers, and he sighed. "You did, but I'm pretty sure it's because you don't feel you're good enough for me because of my god like status at school." I bit down on my lip, holding back laughter. Was he serious?

"I'm pretty sure that's not why I said no," she muttered, a dark look in her eyes.

"It's okay, sweetheart." He flashed a crooked grin. "You don't have to feel inadequate. I don't care what other people think. I like you. I won't accept the answer no to a second date. You and I have something magical." He draped an arm around her shoulder, hugging her against him.

"If by magical you mean imaginary, than yes, we do have something magical." She shook his arm away. "I'm not going out with you again, Jeremiah."

He sighed, setting an elbow on the table and resting his chin in his hand. "You're a strange girl, Bethany. You don't fall all over me like some girls." He watched her a moment, his eyes moving over her. She glared at the blatant way he took in her body. "I think that's partly why I like you. You're a challenge," he spoke, the smile returning to his lips as his eyes moved to meet hers. He leaned in swiftly and kissed her cheek before getting up and moving away.

Bethany's cheeks burned bright red and her eyes were alive with anger. "That egotistical jock!" she hissed. "I can't stand guys like that, and yet! He's the only one to come after me. Some luck I have." She glared at her food. "You're so lucky to be getting to know a guy like Ryan. He is so much better for you than Lex, or other guys like him and Jeremiah."

A smile danced across my lips as I thought of Friday and my date with Ryan. "I'm pretty excited about that, too."

"You should be," she laughed, giving a small shake of her head. "You should ask him if he has any hot relatives that are around his age and have similar personalities." She picked up her empty tray, discarding the garbage and placing the tray on top of the bin.

"I definitely will," I assured her, following her lead. "I'll see if I can set something up this weekend."

She snapped her fingers, spinning on her heel to me. "I have an idea actually."

"Do tell," I encouraged, heading out of the cafeteria.

"I was thinking. Since the senior class usually has a crazy party the week before graduation, that we should throw our own thing. We can invite Ryan and his friends, they seemed nice." I nodded my agreement. "It could be fun and less dangerous than any party one of the seniors could throw."

"My mom would be up for that," I murmured, remembering how many times she'd denied my pleading to go to one of the high school parties. Sometimes they were personal invites, but most of the time it was a general invite to the whole school. She'd never let me go because of all the horror stories she'd heard.

"And I'm sure I could convince my mom to have it at our house," Bethany mused.

I glanced at my watch, noting I had little time to get to class. "We can talk about it at my house tonight," I said, a subtle reminder of the movie night we'd planned.

"Alright sounds good." She nodded.

With a parting wave, we headed off toward our classes. Down the hallway, I caught sight of Lex, leaning against a locker. Cassy was curled against him, a delicate smile on her lips as he pulled her body closer to his own.

My stomach twisted and I averted my eyes from the P.D.A. they were showing. I tried to keep my thoughts away from the other night, when it was me he'd wanted by his side. We hadn't talked since that day, and by the looks of it, he'd easily moved on after I told him to leave. Did it even hurt him to be denied? I wondered if he'd ever had a bruised ego, or broken heart. Turning away, I prepared myself for another boring lecture.

After class, I walked aimlessly down the hallways. Bethany had to run errands, so I was on my own for getting home. I was out of class and heading home early. Pushing open the door that led outside, I was nearly blinded by the sun and was unable to avoid running into the person right outside. "Sorry!"

The guy I'd run into was someone I didn't recognize. But then again, I didn't actually know that many people in my school. He flashed a grin. "No worries, I'm stronger than I look," he replied, the lingering Italian accent influencing his voice.

"Still, I'm really sorry, I should've been more careful," I rambled, feeling heat rise to my cheeks.

He blinked gray eyes at me, amused. He ran a hand through his dark brown hair. "Seriously, it's fine. I'm not hurt, you're not hurt. Things could be worse." He reasoned.

"Still-"

He cut me off with the wave of his hand. "Stop apologizing, really." I frowned. He stuck a hand out. "I'm Desmond, you are?" I was about to answer when someone else spoke up.

"Honeybee," he called. I turned to see Lex coming towards me. I had to give it to him, the boy had good timing. He somehow always managed to come talk to me the moment another guy started to make conversation.

"That's a unique name," Desmond commented, eyebrow raised in curiosity.

"I'm Olivia to everyone else. Honeybee to him," I corrected, pointing towards Lex, who had come up to stand next to me. His eyes stopped on Desmond, a glare forming. *Is he always angry at someone?*

"Hey, Lex," Desmond spoke, crossing his arms over his chest.

"Desmond." Lex held his glare.

I looked between the two of them, some untold tension in the air. "How do you two know each other?"

Desmond glanced at me. "Soccer." His was voice tight.

"Des here has been trying to take over for me since the beginning of the season. Haven't you?" Lex seethed.

"I wouldn't call it taking over. I'm trying to help the team." I looked between the two of them in confusion, wincing when Lex's hold on my arm tightened. The anger directed toward Desmond was unintentionally coming out at me.

"The team's fine," Lex snapped.

Desmond rolled his eyes. "I'm just trying to help."

"You're trying to take my spot as team captain." Lex's hands curled into fists.

"It would help," Desmond said, a smug grin on his face.

"As if." Lex grabbed my arm, pulling me away. "Don't get hit by a truck, Des."

"Same to you," he called cheerfully. "Bye, Olivia." As I was being pulled by Lex, I waved goodbye.

"Don't talk to him, Honeybee," he told me, pulling me toward the parking lot. *Where are we going?*

"And why not? He seems nice enough." I nearly stumbled over the curb. Lex didn't hesitate, or help me right myself. He just continued to stride toward an unknown destination. "By the way, where are we going?" Why were we even talking? We hadn't spoken since the kiss. Maybe our messed up relationship really didn't affect him the way it affected me.

"I'm taking you home. It is way too hot for you to walk." *Well isn't that thoughtful.* "And he's not nice. He's been trying to get my spot as team captain since school started. Don't let the voice fool you, just because he's got an accent doesn't mean he's better."

"But–"

"No buts Honeybee. He's not good enough to be team captain." We got to his car and he unlocked the doors.

"Are you threatened by him?" I cooed, grinning at the idea. I slipped into the car, leaving my door open to relieve some of the stifling heat.

He scoffed. "Yeah right. Desmond has nothing on me."

"I'll be the judge of that. You guys have a game this Saturday right?"

"You can't come if you're going to judge me, Honeybee," he mumbled, searching his pockets for something.

"Yes I can. Besides, I've seen soccer movies. It seems to me that Italian's are always good soccer players," I mused, twisting the end of my hair around my finger.

"That's profiling," he said, looking around the car.

"No it's not," I said in a sing-song voice. The sun glared brightly, warming my skin. I pulled on my sunglasses, watching as Lex went through his backpack.

"Yes is it."

"What are you looking for?" I demanded to know, snatching my purse away from his hands as he went to look through it.

"My phone. I know I had it." He raised his eyebrows, his shoulder propped up. He was acting like I should've known what he was doing.

"You probably left it in the locker room or something." I said, trying to think logically.

He sighed. "I'll be right back." He opened his car door and started back towards the school.

After about five minutes of waiting, I began wondering if he was ever coming back. I was about to call him when I heard chanting coming from the school. I was able to make out the word 'fight'. My pulse quickened and I hurried from the car, reaching the school yard moments later. I gasped at what I saw.

Lex and Desmond were rolling around on the ground, throwing punches and kicks left and right. Everyone was watching or encouraging them. I rolled my eyes at the immaturity of high school students.

Where was someone in charge when I needed them? Did teachers and the principle care at all that two of their students were fighting on the front lawn in the midst of a growing crowd?

"Lex Diamond!" Cassy shrieked. Lex had a hold of Desmond's collar and had his fist about ready to hit him in the face again. "Stop it this instant before you both get suspended. Graduation is two weeks away!" Her words brought a pause to the chanting and the fight. The two boys glared at each other, neither willing to be the first one to step back. "Lex," Cassy seethed, glaring him down.

Lex lowered his fist and pushed Desmond away. I wondered what had happened to make them break out into a fight. The crowd dispersed and almost everyone left. I noticed Desmond spit out some blood. A few cheerleaders went to help him. Cassy took one look at Lex, apparently decided he was fine, and walked away.

It surprised me that she didn't seem to care that he had just been in a fight. Weren't girlfriends supposed to worry about that kind of thing? Lex had a bloody lip and a few scratches. When he saw me, a grimace passed over his features. "I told you to wait in the car."

"No you didn't," I retorted.

"It was implied." He rubbed his jaw, wiping blood away from the cut on his lip.

"Not the point," I muttered. "What the heck just happened? You leave for two minutes, and a fight breaks out?"

"It's not a big deal," Lex insisted, walking past me. I followed after him. "Come on. Let's get out of here before one of the teachers shows up."

We got back to his car and headed home. The ride was quiet, wind whipping my hair around. Lex had turned the radio on, and sunglasses hid his eyes. I had no idea what was on his mind.

He parked in his driveway and turned the car off, but made no move to get out. Deciding he was taking time to think about something, I grabbed my bag and started to open the door.

His hand caught my arm. "Wait." I paused, turning to look at him. His eyes still stared ahead, dead of emotion. "We need to talk about something." He let my arm go and returned his hands to the wheel.

I gulped, taking my hand off the door. "What?" Were we going to talk about the other night? It seemed like a lot of our conversations revolved around his kissing me.

His jaw tightened, hands gripping the wheel so tightly his knuckles turned white. "I...I didn't mean for this to happen." Dark eyes peeked at me a millisecond before turning away.

"I don't understand," I breathed, dropping my bag to the floor again.

He slid his hands from the wheel, his arm moving to rest on the back of the seat. If he moved much closer, his fingers would brush across the skin of my neck. "I'm sorry... about the other night." His jaw clenched again, like he was fighting with himself. "I shouldn't have kissed you, again." My chest constricted, and no words would come out; not that I had any idea what to say. "And I'm sorry you saw the fight today. It seems I can't control myself lately." He leaned his head back, eyes closed.

My breathing was shallow, and I couldn't describe the feeling I was having. It was a mixture of butterflies that had undoubtedly turned into zombies and were thus wreaking havoc on my insides.

I felt sick. "Lex, I…"

He shook his head, leaning up. "Don't say anything. Knowing you, you'll find a way to apologize or justify my stupid, impulsive behavior, and I'm not looking for that. Just know I'm sorry, and it won't happen again." He turned toward me, eyes full of sincerity. "I promise."

My breath seemed to rush back in when he got out of the car. My chest heaved up and down, trying to regain a sense of stability. Pushing the door, I left the car and headed across the street, his words playing over in my head. Was it a good thing that he would never kiss me again? It was. So why did I feel so sad?

Chapter Fourteen – Friendly Fighters

A horn outside made me hurry out of the kitchen. "Bye, Mom!" I called, moving out of the door and heading toward Bethany's car. Lex was across the street, throwing his things in the back of his jeep. He lifted a wave in acknowledgement. I smiled before hopping into the car.

"About time, I've been ready for ten minutes," Bethany mumbled, backing out of the driveway. "I can't be late again. Knowing my luck, I'll get caught this time."

We were pulling into school a few minutes early when someone honked behind us. I turned, seeing Jeremiah send a wink Bethany's way. She replied with a glare, pulling into a parking spot. "I seriously can't stand it. He's become even more of a nuisance now that I've hardcore rejected him."

"Poor dear," I murmured, grabbing my bag.

As she exited the car, she huffed, mumbling something about me being inconsiderate to her feelings. I grinned, moving inside the school. The heat inside the building almost outdid the heat outside. The bodies clustered together, each moving slowly to their destinations.

Bethany stopped inside the door and stared with dead eyes at the crowd in front of us. "I hate high school."

"One more week," I murmured, giving a small smile of encouragement.

"If only words were enough to suffice," she sighed, saluting before heading off. I smirked and moved through the mass of students. They laughed, making jokes to each other as they went. A group of guys tossed a football toward their teammate, one of which ran into me. I stumbled to the side, glaring as he retreated toward his friends, oblivious to the person he'd just run over. *I hate high school, too.*

When homeroom rolled around, I wasn't excited. I was even more upset when Lex walked in. His face lit up in a mischievous smile as he bee-lined my way. I noticed the light bruising and split lip, marks from the fight with Desmond.

Lex smiled. "Hello, Honeybee." I raised an eyebrow when he dropped his things on the floor, slipping into the seat next to me. "It's good to see me."

"What?" I twisted my neck to look at him, an eyebrow raised in confusion.

"I'm voicing your thoughts," he supplied, pulling out his books, resting his legs on the edge of the table. I'd never realized how long his legs were, but I supposed being a soccer player, having long legs helped somewhat. "You shouldn't stare, it's not polite." Heat spread across my cheeks. He chuckled lightly.

"Aren't you in the wrong row?" I mumbled, pushing my glasses back up.

He shrugged, glancing at the back of the room. "No, I'm right where I want to be." Why did he have to be so confusing? It was exhausting.

"Are you now?" I breathed, crossing my ankles. He nodded, and looked like he was about to reply when someone cleared their throat in front of us. Looking up, I felt relieved. It was like manna from heaven. "Bethany!"

"Hi," she said curtly, glaring daggers at Lex. He gasped, holding his hands out in question. "What are you doing here?"

"Why are you angry that I'm here?"

"We both know who you are, therefore my caution is completely understandable," she retorted. "Besides, that's my chair. Move along, now."

"There isn't assigned seating in here, Bridges. It's first come, first serve." He glanced around the room. "There are plenty of other seats. You should go find one before the old lady gets in," he suggested. Almost on cue, the sound of clicking heels penetrated the hallway as Mrs. Bitsley parted the crowd. Being the principal's wife, everyone moved out of her way for fear of being wrongly imprisoned in detention.

"Seriously, Lex. Move." Bethany's glare seemed to blaze with annoyance the longer he stared up at her, a smirk painted across his face.

"Lex," I mumbled. He glanced sideways at me, but didn't reply.

Mrs. Bitsley's plump form walked through the doorway, her once dark hair dusted with gray was tied in a knot on top of her head. Her floral dress was blaring with bright colors, dark frames resting on her nose. Her dark eyes immediately picked up on Bethany's still standing form. "Ms. Bridges, please take a seat," her voice was rough from years of smoking. Bethany sent one more glare at Lex before taking one of the seats behind us. I sighed, denying the urge to slam my hands on the table in protest.

Mrs. Bitsley turned to the papers on her desk. She also taught one of the foreign languages and was probably grading papers. The rest of the class settled into quiet chatter, working on different things to pass the time.

I turned around in my seat to look at Bethany. She took a break from burning holes in the back of Lex's head to look at me. "I hate him," she mouthed, rolling her eyes.

I laughed, and nodded my head. My agreement was a contradiction to how my heart felt every time I caught a whiff of his cologne, or saw his face light up with a smile. I couldn't ignore the spark of electricity that went through me whenever he brushed by, or the way my breathing became rapid and shallow when my thoughts wandered to our shared kisses.

Sighing, I groaned internally for letting my thoughts focus on Lex again. I needed to get away from him, focus on other things for a while. I glanced at Bethany. "I think I should move to Mars." My words quieted when I noticed the way Lex's ears tweaked back at the sound.
"What about me?" She feigned hurt. "I suppose I would have to stay here alone?"

I shook my head. "You'd come, too. No way would I leave you here alone. You'd get bored without me," I predicted with a grin.

"That's true. Plus, there are probably a lot of alien boys up there. I might fall in love," she reasoned, weighing the pros of moving to Mars with me.

"Do you think alien guys are cute?" I asked with a grin.

She giggled and pushed my shoulder. "Honestly, you're such a child sometimes."

"It's a valid question. Are aliens cute or not?" I really *was* curious now.

She slapped my shoulder. "Shush, it's not a valid question at all." She glanced at the front of the class.

"It will be when I move to Mars," I murmured, feigning superiority.

"You're moving to Mars? And you didn't even tell me?" Lex mocked.

I sat up and glared at him. "I wasn't talking to you, so buzz off."

"That's what you do, Honeybee," he chuckled.

"Quiet." The word was spat at us from the front of the class. Mrs. Bitsley glared at the three of us, her eyes narrowing in on me. I wanted to throw my hands up and demand what I had done, but that would only further enrage her.

Lex grinned at me, noting the way I was singled out. "You're such a bad kid, Bee."

"I am not!" I stated a little louder than intended.

"Ms. Martin," Mrs. Bitsley seethed, glowering at me. Seriously? Was she blinded by Lex's good looks as well? Or did she have something against me? I frowned, sitting forward in my seat, arms crossed.

Lex stretched his arms out, hiding a yawn behind a hand. "You're cute when you're angry." I willed my cheeks to hide the blush I felt. He leaned closer. "And even cuter when you blush," he whispered, his lips brushing my skin.

In retrospect, I shouldn't have been blamed for what happened. It was a knee-jerk reaction, shoving him as hard as I could away from me. I didn't expect to be so strong and send him flying from his chair onto the floor, where he would accidentally send one of the potted plants toppling over.

A few of the girls in the class bolted from their chairs and rushed to Lex's aid, while Mrs. Bitsley huffed, leaving her chair to come stand in front of me. I shrunk back in my chair, willing her to have momentary brain damage and forget what had just happened.

"Ms. Martin, that is quite enough! You're interrupting class, and beating up fellow students!" Behind me, I heard Bethany choke on her laughter.

I bit my lip hard to keep from chuckling with her. "I'm sorry, Mrs. Bitsley, it was an accident I swear–"

"Go to the office." Her cold words sent a shiver down my back. *The office*? I gulped. "Now," she said the word slowly, dragging it out so the whole class could hear her words. I picked up my bag and left the room, stealing a glance back at Bethany, who sat rigid in her chair. She looked worried. She wasn't the only one.

I cringed when Bethany slapped my shoulder in shock. "You got detention?" she demanded to know as we walked to the Detention hall. *Hall*. Not just room, hall. How many rule breakers did we have in this school?

"Yeah. I called Mom and left her a message telling her what happened. She'll probably have a decent amount to say when I get home. And I texted Ryan. He's meeting me around six instead of five."

"Well at least he still wants to go out with you. After all, you are one of the bad kids now," she joked, trying to lighten the mood. "Come on, it's not so bad. It's just one day. Don't stress it." She smiled.

"I'll try," I said. We stopped outside the Detention hall. She wished me good luck before heading home. I took a deep breath and walked into the hall.

One of the teachers was sitting at a desk in the front. There were papers all over his desk, and a coffee cup in his hand. I glanced around and saw scattered groups of students doing homework, throwing paper airplanes at each other. The fact they looked like they weren't having a horrible time really messed with my preconceived notion of what detention was like.

I stood still, not knowing what to do. This *was* my first time. The teacher looked up and saw me standing there. He waved me over. "Are you looking for me? Or someone in detention?" He thought I was lost?

"No, I'm here to serve my time," I murmured gravely. "I've never had detention before, so I don't know how this works." My cheeks were probably rosy with embarrassment.

The teacher almost laughed. "Well then, welcome to detention. I'm Mr. Lowch, though the regulars here call me Jay. Just take a seat wherever, you can do homework if you want. But, as you can see, most of the kids just sit around and wait. It's too bad you did something bad alone. It's more fun for the kid's to do stuff together so they can talk about if in here after they're caught. " He smiled.

I was almost sad that I'd been such a good student. Mr. Lowch seemed like a nice guy. Plus he was so laid back, it seemed like detention was no big deal at all.

"Okay, thanks."

"No problem. Oh, one thing though, electronics aren't allowed. And if I see you using one, I get to confiscate it until the end of the period. So watch it."

"I will. Thanks." I walked over to where no one was sitting and pulled out some extra math homework and began to work on the problems. I was minding my own business when someone ran into my chair, almost knocking me out of it. I looked up annoyed at the person's clumsiness.

"Well, well, well. What are the odds of literally bumping into you again?" Desmond wondered, a smirk on his lips.

"I have no idea. But of course it had to happen here." I grumbled, going to pick up my pencil, which had flown from my fingers when Desmond had almost knocked me over. I noticed the fresh blood on his chin with disdain.

He sat down in the chair next to me. He was glancing around at the other groups of people. He waved at a few different people before returning his attention to me. "So, what are you in for?"

"Interrupting class and beating up a fellow student," I managed to say with a serious face. "And you?"

He looked me over, as if to size me up. "If I didn't know better, I wouldn't believe you." What did he mean by that? "And I got into another fight." He shrugged. "I might've accidentally on purpose broken his nose." I gaped. "But it's not a big deal. A nose job might help the kid get a date." He chewed on his lip a moment. "If I don't get a thank you card I'm going to be a little upset, actually."

"That is terrible!" I cried out, shaking my head in disbelief. People thought I was violent for shoving Lex out of his chair on *accident*. Desmond found humor in breaking someone's nose.

He grinned. "Almost as terrible as what I heard happened in class."

I raised an eyebrow. If he was talking about what happened with Lex, it wasn't that terrible. "What do you mean?"

"I heard that the notorious Honeybee, the girl from Lex Diamond's past, finally broke down and beat him over the head with a chair. This happened only moments before she tried to harvest his organs for her own witchy reasons, which I think had something to do with recreating Lex clones and having cyborg babies," he mumbled, shrugging carelessly.

I gaped, gripping the edges of the desk tightly. "W-what?" How was it possible something like that could spread so quickly and get so out of control and downright crazy in a matter of hours?

He nodded, running a hand through his dark hair, smoothing out some of the curls. "You heard me. You went from being his creepy next door neighbor, to the girl who tried to have his cyborg babies. Talk about an upgrade." He smirked, sarcasm dripping from his tone.

"Desmond, are they seriously saying that?" He nodded. I groaned, putting my head in my hands. "Thank goodness there is only a week and a half left of school!"

"Amen to that, sister." He pulled an energy drink from his backpack, snapping the top back and taking a drink. "But for what it's worth, I'm sure you two would make hot cyborg babies."

I glared, my lips set in a firm line. "Shut. Up."

He laughed, wiping away the moisture from the side of his lips. "Sorry," he murmured. "However, I'm proud someone other than me finally beat that guy up and put him in his place. He's so arrogant."

"I've known him most of my life, arrogant is an understatement," I told him, leaning my elbow on the table, the rumor still tumbling around in my head.

"You poor thing," he mumbled, patting my shoulder. I smirked, laying my arms across the desk and setting my head down. "For what it's worth, I'm sad I wasn't the one to beat him up so badly that I ended up getting myself detention."

I groaned, closing my eyes momentarily. "I didn't even mean to beat him up!" I turned my head to look at him. "I just don't know my own strength, that's all."

Desmond chuckled, leaning back in his chair, stretching his tall and muscular frame. "Sure, because after years of being the butt of every joke he tells, what could ever possess you to want to beat him up?" I frowned. He had a point. "Which is why his behavior is so strange," he said more to himself than to me.

I raised an eyebrow, and prodded his arm. "What are you talking about?"

He hesitated, his lips parted with an explanation on the tip of his tongue. "Umm."

"Just tell me," I mumbled, sitting up straighter.

"Fine." He glanced around a moment before letting the words spill from his lips. "I kind of thought you two had some secret affair going on, and he covers it up with insults and stuff. I mean, he is not shy about telling us to back off his next door neighbor."

I burst out laughing, gaining the attention of many of the students spending their afternoon in detention. Even Mr. Lowch glanced my way, raising an eyebrow in question.

When my laugher was under control, I looked at Desmond, wiping my eyes. "That's the funniest thing I've heard in a while." My breathing was rapid. "There is no way Lex and I have a secret affair. We can hardly be in the same room together without something bad happening."

"Define bad." He waggled his eyebrows suggestively, effectively putting an end to my laughter.

"Shut up." I glowered. "Can we talk about something else?"

He grinned in triumph, like he'd discovered some dark secret. Hopefully he didn't assume his hypothesis was correct, and go around telling people Lex and I were secretly together. That would create all sorts of havoc. "As you wish."

For the rest of detention we talked about random things. I didn't get any homework done, but I learned Desmond and I had more in common than I'd thought. We both loved ice cream and Oreos. And he wasn't afraid to admit that he liked romance movies. Perhaps I could find a friend in him. Even if he thought it was funny my reputation was becoming even more humiliating.

"Go home and enjoy your weekend." Mr. Lowch said, packing up his own bag and papers.

Desmond and I walked outside into the lovely afternoon weather. "Well, it's been nice getting to know you," he said.

"And you as well."

"I'll see you around, Olivia," he said, heading off towards his car which was parked near the front.

"Bye, Desmond." I called back, walking home. After all, I had a date to get ready for.

Chapter Fifteen – Date with a fro-yo boy

At exactly 6:03pm the doorbell rang. Grinning, I moved toward the door. My black flats slapped against the wooden flooring until I came to a stop in front of the mirror to make sure I looked okay before I opened the door.

The snug white skinny jeans made my legs seem longer. A forest green shirt with short sleeves and a v-neck contrasted well with my jeans. My hair was down, and my glasses stood out brightly. With a deep breath, I opened the door.

"Hey," Ryan greeted with a smiled. He was wearing dark jeans and a dark gray t-shirt with a small mustache sewn into the pocket on his shirt. His dark hair was messy, like he'd just run his hand through it in attempt to calm it down.

"Hi," I replied.

"You look great," he said, taking in my appearance.

I blushed. "Thanks. So do you."

"Ready to go?" he asked, the ever present smile on his face. It made all the butterflies wake up.

"Yeah, where are we going?" I asked, grabbing my purse and black cardigan. I followed his lead.

"If I told you, it would ruin the surprise. Wouldn't want that now would we?" he asked, unlocking the car.

"Surprise huh? That doesn't sound good." I got into the car and waited for him to walk around the front and get in the driver's side.

He opened the door and slid into his seat. "Don't worry. I'm not taking you to a really expensive restaurant and proposing or anything. It's a small surprise that won't likely cause you any physical, emotional, or mental harm," he finished with a smirk. I was still frowning, not sure what to expect. He turned towards me. "The surprise works best if you wear this." He produced a blindfold.

"What if you take me out to the middle of nowhere and murder me or something?" I gasped. His smirk disappeared and he looked at me for a moment in silence. "The surprise isn't me dying, right?" I feigned disappointment.

He chuckled, starting the car. "No, I'm not going to murder you, don't worry. Now put on the blindfold, okay?"

"Why can't you tell me what the surprise is?" He turned to look at me, eyebrows raised. I sighed, defeated. He handed it to me, and I wrapped it around my head, covering my eyes. "There. Let's go." He started the car and I felt it moving away.

It was kind of weird being blind in the car. I had to completely trust him in his driving. I couldn't see a thing. "Are we almost there? This is creeping me out." I felt the car turning.

"Blind people do this all the time," he reminded me, "And yes, we're almost there."

"Just in case you didn't realize, I'm not blind," I told him. The car stopped momentarily before going again. t was probably a stop sign.

"The way you checked me out when I picked you up told me as much," he teased. I blushed embarrassed. "Don't worry, Olivia, I checked you out, too."

I turned in the direction I thought he was. "Well good! I had a hard time deciding what to wear and how to do my makeup. You have no idea how hard it is to be a girl."

"No I don't, but the end product is really pretty."

That made me blush again. "Thanks."

Within about ten minutes, the car stopped and he turned off the engine. I heard the car door open and shut. I gaped. Was he really leaving me in the car? I nearly jumped when the door next to me opened.

He laughed. "Calm down, I'm just helping you out, I don't need you tripping." He helped me out of the car, safely, and he led me somewhere.

"Are we almost there?" I whined. "I'm worried you really are going to kill me."

"Would you relax? I'm not going to kill you. We're in a public place." Like that would calm me down.

"Seriously, Ryan. If you don't let me take this blindfold off, I might freak out or something." I mumbled.

"Olivia, if you flip out it might put a damper on the sweet thing I'm trying to do."

I frowned and crossed my arms across my chest. "Rude." He laughed at my comment, and continued to lead me somewhere. I could hear the people around us, there were *lots* of them.

"Ryan..." I mumbled.

"We're almost there."

"Fine." I groaned.

We continued walking, and I heard the whispered words of people who saw us walking around, wondering what we were doing and why I had a blindfold on. I was right there with them. I had no idea why there was a blindfold on my head. But supposedly, I would know soon enough.

"Hey Ryan," a man said. His words were followed by a short laugh. "Is this the girl?"

"Yeah," Ryan laughed. "Jon Paul, this is Olivia."

"Nice to meet you," he greeted.

"I'd say the same, but for all I know you're helping him murder me and hide my body."

The other person laughed again. "Don't worry, babe. Ryan's got a nice night planned for you."

Ryan moved forward, and I heard the *ding* of an elevator. When the doors opened, we stepped on. Since I was already unsteady from being blindfolded, I leaned closer to him when the elevator moved. A few moments later the doors opened and the breeze caressed my skin softly. We walked out of the elevator, his arm carefully guiding me. "You ready to take the blindfold off?"

I scoffed. "Like you even have to ask."

His hands were at the back of my head, untying the blindfold. A few seconds later, my vision returned. My breath hitched as I took in my surroundings.

We were on a rooftop. A table and two chairs were set up, not far from where we were standing, along with a picnic basket dinner. The white table cloth flittered in the breeze. I glanced to the side and saw the ocean sparkling in the distance. The sun was glittering against the faraway beaches, starting its descent. It was a sunset dinner on a rooftop, and it was a beautiful.

"What do you think?" he asked, glancing away nervously.

"Ryan, it's beautiful." I was awestruck he would do this for a first date. "Really, thank you for taking me up here."

"You're welcome, Olivia. I wanted this to be special," he sounded unsure of himself, and I wanted to make him more sure of himself. Show him, that it meant a lot to me.

"Ryan, this is my first ever date," I told him, squeezing his hand gently. "It is special." I kissed his cheek.

"Good. I'm glad."

"When did you set this all up?" I wondered as he led me over to the small table set up.

"This afternoon. I got this part all set up, and my mother helped me with the food actually." He handed me some of the food. "It's actually because of your little mishap at school that I had time to get everything set up, and she even made us desert."

I took the first bite, and my taste buds sang Hallelujah choruses. "This is amazing."

"I'll be sure to tell her as much," he chuckled. "I guess it's good you're one of the bad kids, huh?" he winked. I grinned, looking forward to the rest of the evening.

We stayed on the roof watching the sun set for another hour or so, and it was so romantic. There was a bench on the roof, and he'd brought a blanket up earlier, so we huddled underneath the blanket when the temperature started to drop. It was around nine o'clock when we decided it was time to head home.

The drive was peaceful, and I still had a smile lingering on my lips from all the thought he'd put into our date. It was so sweet. When we reached my house he walked me to the door.

"Thank you, Ryan." I said, looking up to meet his eyes. "That was the best date I've ever been on." I shivered, pulling my cardigan closer around me.

"One for the history books I'm sure," he leaned in and kissed my cheek. "I'll call you," he said.

"You'd better. You don't go on a date with a girl and then not call. Especially because I know where you work." I winked.

"That would be kind of awkward," he laughed.

"Most definitely." I reached up and hugged him, his arms wrapping around my waist to return the hug.

"Goodnight, Ryan." I whispered.

We let go and he grabbed my hand, kissing it lightly. "Goodnight, Olivia. Sleep well." He started walking backwards towards his car.

"Same to you," I said, opening the door. I waited for him to drive away before I shut the door. I leaned against it, smiling to myself.

Best date ever.

Chapter Sixteen – Surprise!

Saturday morning came around with something I really didn't want to hear.

"We're going on a camping trip!" Mom shouted happily as she walked into my room, pulling open the curtains and turning back towards me. I mumbled something incoherent and pulled my covers farther over my head.

"Olivia Rayne Martin!" A voice sang.

I sat bolt right up in bed and felt the blood drain from my face. There, standing across from me and holding my stuffed blue penguin, was none other than Lex Diamond. The night after my date with Ryan, and Lex was the first person I had to see.

Fantastic.

"Mom." She was standing near the window still. "What on earth is going on here?" I demanded to know, glaring quickly at Lex. He smiled at me and started to pet Froofie's little blue head.

"Well, Patty and I were talking yesterday, and we thought this is the last week before you two kids graduate. So, we're going to take a weekend trip camping as a family one last time."

"And we're both being forced to come." Lex told me, tossing Mom a look.

"We're leaving in less than two hours. You need to pack. We're spending the night, so pack for tonight and tomorrow. Don't pack your cellphone, that's your punishment for getting sent to detention," she said, starting to move towards the door. She stopped and turned back to me. "Oh and by the way, I want to know all about your date with Ryan last night." She winked before leaving me alone in the room with Lex. It was weird she had no issues when we were alone together. But if Ryan was alone with me, she went on red alert.

Lex glanced back at me. "So that was Ryan who dropped you off last night."

I nodded, throwing back my covers and getting out of my bed. I was glad I'd worn P.J. pants and a tank instead of underwear and a t-shirt like I sometimes did when it was hot. "Yep, that was him."

"So how was it?" he asked casually, sitting down on my bed.

I searched around in my drawers for something to wear. "Um, why does it matter to you?" I asked, grabbing a pair of white short shorts out and tossing them at my bed. I heard a slight mumble from behind me. I turned and tried to suppress a laugh when I saw the shorts were draped over his face. "Sorry." The urge to giggle almost won.

"I can tell," he mumbled, moving the shorts off of his face. "And it doesn't really matter to me. I'm just curious."

Rolling my eyes, I started searching for a top. Why did he want to know about Ryan? So he could make fun of me? Say our date was silly or something? I didn't want him to mock me anymore.

"Honeybee," he said, "I'm sort of waiting for you to respond here."

"I don't really want to tell you," I said, leaning against my dresser. Lex twisted his baseball cap around so the bill was at the back of his head. He had on black shorts and a vibrant blue t-shirt. I probably looked hideous in return, with bed head and wrinkled pajamas.

"Can I guess?" He moved to the middle of my bed, Froofie in his lap. I shrugged my shoulders. "It's either now or later on today when we're sitting around the campfire and your mom asks you for the details."

I grabbed an orange V-neck, while discreetly grabbing a bra and underwear, and walked towards the bed, snatching my shorts. "Don't you have packing to do or something?"

"My parents hate me. They made me get up two hours ago to pack," he muttered, playing with Froofie in his hands.

"They woke you up before ten on a Saturday?" I gasped, feigning horror.

"Yeah, parents these days. Anyways, so I'm here to help you pack. You're definitely going to want to bring that bikini of yours." He waggled his eyebrows.

I glared at him. "Pig." I slammed the bathroom door. I stripped out of my pajamas, and pulled on the clothes I'd grabbed. I threw my hair up into a messy ponytail, letting my bangs frame my face, and applied a little makeup before slipping on my glasses.

I opened my door and gasped upon seeing Lex going through my drawers. "Lex!" I screamed, moving over towards my purple dresser, and shoving him away. "What do you think you're doing?"

"I'm helping you get ready to go," he replied. He smiled innocently at me and even tried to use Froofie against me. He moved Froofie in front of his face and started talking a high pitched voice. "Honeybee, please don't be mad at Lex. He was just trying to be helpful." His Froofie voice got me.

I started giggling, and I saw his childlike smile from behind Froofie's head. "I hate you."

He laughed. "My mother is downstairs. She has breakfast. You should go down and eat." He set Froofie down on the bed.

"Okay, I'll be down in a few minutes. I'm gonna throw some stuff in a bag for this stupid trip."

"Do you need help?"

"No-" I started to say.

"Okay, I'll pack for you." He pushed me out of the room, shutting and locking the door behind me.

I groaned, slamming on the door with my fist. "Lex! This isn't funny. Let me in!"

"I'm packing for you, deal with it." I could almost hear the smirk in his words. "Go eat, Bee." he instructed. I stomped my foot in frustration and went downstairs.

Patty was sitting at the table, a plate of pancakes in front of her. She smiled when she saw me. "Morning Livie, how are you?" she asked, pouring me a cup of orange juice.

"Fine. This trip sure was a surprise though," I said, taking a sip, feeling the cool liquid slide down my throat.

"It's long overdue," she replied, dishing me up some eggs and a pancake.

"Thanks." I smiled.

"Anytime, hon," she cooed, turning to dish up some more food. I heard the front door open and the sound of footsteps making their way into the kitchen. Steve appeared, dressed in khaki shorts and a floral button down shirt, looking ready for a day off. He also looked like one of those retired golfers. "We've got our stuff loaded. The only bag we're waiting on is Livie's. The rest of the sleeping bags and tents are all loaded up," he said, smiling at me in greeting.

"Where's your bag, Olivia?" Mom asked, blowing on her coffee.

I scratched my head, somewhat embarrassed. "Umm ... Lex is packing for me."

Two hours later we were all packed together in Steve's truck, our stuff in the back. I'd called Bethany and Ryan and told them what was going on. They were both a bit worried about me going on a trip with Lex, but I assured them it would be okay.

Mom was sitting up front with Patty and Steve. Lex and I were in the back. He was texting on his phone, while I stared longingly out the window, wishing Mom had allowed me to bring my phone. I was bored and my iPod was packed away where I couldn't get it. Stupid Lex and his packing skills. Or lack thereof.

"So, Olivia, are you excited about graduating?" Patty asked, turning slightly in her leather seat to see me better. Lex glanced up at the sound of someone speaking, but quickly returned his eyes to his fancy phone.

"Yes." I smiled.

"I remember when I graduated, feels like it was just yesterday," she remembered with a laugh. "Steve, do you remember?"

He winked at her. "I do, it was a night of amazing memories," he said with a certain tone, wiggling his eyebrows.

Lex glanced up in time to see the eyebrow show and looked between his parents a moment. The facial expression he pulled made me laugh. His eyes got huge, eyebrows scrunched together, and his jaw dropped. "Mom, dad, please tell me you're not talking about ..." He trailed off, his cheeks slightly tinted. He always blushed when his parents were romantic, or talked about romance in front of him. It was kind of adorable and reminded me of when he was younger and innocent.

Patty rolled her eyes. "Good grief, Lex. You act like that's unheard of, but no. That was the night your father first said he loved me," she said, smirking at how Lex's face instantly relaxed, and he breathed a sigh of relief.

"Thank goodness. Honeybee's ears are too innocent for such talk," he said, giving me a sympathetic look.

"She's not as innocent as you think," Mom said, glancing at me in the rear view mirror. I crinkled my nose trying to figure out what she meant by that.

"Oh, is little Livie growing up to fast?" Patty asked, encouraging Mom to go on.

"Well, just the other night when I had to work late, I came back home and she was sitting on the couch all cozy with Ryan watching a movie."

"Awh, that's so sweet," Patty said, smiling back at me. "That sounds like something we did when we first started dating," she said, glancing towards Steve. He smiled and slid his hand against her cheek.

"Indeed it does," he replied.

Lex gagged. "Gross, go on with Honeybee's story, I'd rather hear that. It doesn't make me want to throw up."

"Get a grip, Lex." Steve said to his son, looking at him in the rearview mirror. Lex glared back until his dad looked away.

"Anyways," Mom said, trying to get past the tension between the two. "After they watched a movie, they went into her bedroom and shut the door."

"I did not," I claimed, sitting forwards in the seat. "You know that I left it open,"

"A crack," she said, rolling her eyes. "Like that's going to help much."

"Didn't stop you from bursting in,"

"Go Mama bee," Lex said, smirking in my general direction.

"Thank you, Lex." She laughed. "I didn't catch them doing anything, but they did go on a date last night, so who knows what those two lovebirds did. Nothing inappropriate, I'm sure," she murmured, adding a threatening edge to her voice. I blushed, feeling everyone's attention on me.

"Well, are you gonna prove yourself innocent? Or let the minds of married people work their dark magic?" Lex questioned, slipping his phone into his pocket.

"I guess I'd better talk," I decided, taking a deep breath. "Well, he came and picked me up at six, and he blindfolded me."

"He kidnapped you?!" Lex mocked, eyes wide and jaw lowered.

I frowned at him before continuing. "Anyways," I muttered pointedly and continued to tell them the overview of the night before. During my story, both Mom and Patty were smiling, even Steve seemed to approve. Lex looked indifferent, but I was pretty sure I'd seen him tense up during my recap of the date.

"Oh, Livie, that sounds like a wonderful date." Patty smiled.

"It does," Mom agreed.

"He's a really good guy," I replied. In the corner of my eye, I saw Lex's features harden, as he turned to glare out the window.

"Your dad probably would've waited up with a shotgun until you got home and ruined any chance of a goodnight kiss," Mom murmured, smiling sadly.

My heart ached a little at those words. Dad wouldn't be there to meet any boyfriends, my husband, and my children would never know him. I sucked in a breath sharply to keep the emotion from my face.

"Speaking of which, did he?" Patty asked, with a sly grin on her face.

I raised an eyebrow in confusion. "What are you talking about?"

"I mean did he kiss you goodnight?" she asked.

I froze. Either I told them the truth, and risked Patty feeling sad for me because, for all I knew, she didn't know about my first kiss. Or I lied just to see Lex's reaction, *if* he even had a reaction. Curiosity got the better of me.

"Umm ... yeah, he did." I said, shyly looking down, while glancing towards Lex. His jaw clenched and he popped a few knuckles. He reached towards his bag, searching a moment before he grabbed his iPod to tune us out.

"Oh!" Mom said, "Olivia, why didn't you say anything?" she asked, smiling. "I would've wanted to know that when you got home."

"I didn't want to bother you," I replied, glancing away again.

"What was it like?" Patty gushed.

"Oh, um, it was ..." I started, trying to think. My brain went back to the tree house, those years earlier. The feelings of Lex kissing me for the first time flooded my head, and I could almost sense that same I-feel-like-passing-out-this-is-so-amazing feeling running through me. My lips started going before I knew what I was saying. "It was perfect." I said. "Unexpected, sweet, and not like anything I'd imagined it would be..." I trailed off. "It's probably the best first kiss ever."

Lex jerked his head up, even though he was supposedly listening to music. "Best, huh?"

Mom shot me a look, obviously knowing what he was trying to imply. Even Patty seemed to understand what he was hinting at. Maybe Lex was right, and Mom told Patty about the first kiss he and I shared.

"Yes," I replied. He turned away and stared out the window, not giving a response.

"That's sweet, honey," Mom said softly.

Patty nodded her agreement. "And don't mind Lex. He doesn't know what it's like to kiss a girl he really cares about. The boy only dates those popular chicks, plastic. Nobody real." she said. I'd heard her talk about this before to him. She really didn't like the girls he dated.

"Whatever," I said, shrugging it off and smiling. "He can mope if he wants. We're going to have fun today."

"Yes we are," Mom agreed, smiling. "Celebrating the last weekend when you kids are still in high school."

"I can't believe they've grown up so fast," Patty sighed, as the two of them turned back to the front, talking about how much we'd changed over the past eighteen years. I smiled, and turned to look out the window, watching the scenery fly by.

Chapter Seventeen – Rckindling

Around three o'clock that afternoon, we made it to the campground, and the men set to work to put the tents up. I was sitting on a picnic table eating from a bag of marshmallows. The table wasn't very comfortable. I'd already gotten two splinters in my hand and whined quite loudly when Mom used the tweezers to gct them out.

I glanced up at the lovely weather we were having. The sun still beat down on us warmly, glinting off the lake we were camped next to. A cool breeze came off of the water and made the temperature practically perfect. The trees loomed above us, and the brush added a wildlife feel to the area, even though we were only a few hours away from home.

My attention was pulled away from the scenery when I heard my name.

"Honeybee, those are for tonight's bonfire, you can't eat them all now. What am I going to use for smores?" Lex demanded to know, hands on his hips.

"You could always pout. Maybe a fellow camper will pity you and give you some," I proposed.

He rolled his eyes at me, zipping the tent closed. "Yeah, that's a great idea."

"I thought so, too," I said with a cheesy grin.

He snatched the bag of marshmallows from my hands. "No more." He took the bag with him when he went to go help his dad with the other tent.

I watched as Mom and Patty talked on inside the car like it had never stopped. They'd started talking about someone at Mom's work, who she apparently thought was handsome. Needless to say, I'd tuned out the conversation the moment it started. I knew it was natural for her to notice other men, but it still seemed weird to me. She was old. She wasn't supposed to notice *that* anymore. She wasn't supposed to notice anyone after Dad.

"Dad, you're doing it wrong!" Lex groaned, glaring at his father.

"Well! Then why don't you do it? You seem to have a better understanding on setting up tents than I do!" Steve yelled, throwing the tent down and walking away. He walked down the paved road and off towards the lake.

Lex was muttering to himself while trying to put the tent together. I hopped off the table and started over to him. He glared at the tent, oblivious to the fact I was coming over.

"Lex," I said, catching his attention.

"What?" he snapped, getting one of the tents put together.

"You need help. So you and me," I said, gesturing between the two of us. "We're going to talk about your daddy issues."

His face hardened. "No thanks."

"We are," I continued in a sing-song voice.

"Not." He moved away from me so he didn't have to listen to me. I rolled my eyes and groaned. We would talk about his daddy issues whether he liked it or not. I'd tie him down and sit on him till he talked. We might not have been great friends, and he hurt me more than he knew, but I still cared about that stupid jerk, and I wanted to help him.

Later that night, our parents left us alone and went for a walk around the lake. For wanting to enjoy a last weekend with us, they weren't really spending very much time together with their kids. I sighed, glancing across the fireplace where Lex was roasting a marshmallow.

"Stop staring, it's freaking me out." He didn't even look up when he spoke. His dark eyes glowed, the sparks of the fire making his green irises looked hazel.

"I'm bored," I moped, my shoulders drooping forward. "You're not talking. I don't have a phone, so I'm bored."

"I'm so sorry you don't have your *boyfriend* to talk to," he muttered.

I rolled my eyes. "We went on one date. I don't know what we are yet." He gave a humorless laugh. "And I already know you don't like him, so you don't need to remind me."

"If you know I don't like Ryan, then why date him? If Bethany didn't like him, you wouldn't date him. What's so different about me not liking him?" he questioned quietly. I looked up startled. That was unexpected. He sat, staring at me as he waited for an answer.

"I don't know how to answer that," I stammered.

"Honestly." His eyes were like daggers, they pierced my heart.

I sighed. "We're not friends anymore." I didn't make eye contact. "After the past four years, everything that's happened, do you honestly think I would consult you on who I date?" I glanced up at him. He was once again staring into the fire pit. His jaw was working back and forth, like he was trying to control his emotions. "You broke my trust over and over again. What would possess me to tell you anything, or ask your opinion on anything?" I continued.

"I thought you might still care about my opinion." He shrugged. "After being friends for so long, I thought maybe when it came to decisions like dating you might want to talk to someone who knows you."

"Like you consulted me for all of the girls you dated?" I retorted, trying to keep the edge from my voice.

"Maybe if I had, I wouldn't have been such a heartbreaker." He tossed another log onto the fire, sending embers flying into the air. The wind caught them and pulled them around, making the embers look like fireflies.

"This all revolves around the choices you made to get to this point, Lex," I told him, wrapping my sweater tighter over my shoulders.

"I know," he grumbled, running a hand through his hair. "I hate that I ruined our friendship, I really do. I wish I could take it all back. So we were still best friends, and you could trust me."

"Well, you can't." I took another marshmallow from the bag, stuffing it into my mouth.

"If I could, would you let me?" he asked, looking from the fire to me. "Would you want to be my friend after all I've done?"

"What are you talking about?" I mumbled around the marshmallow, thoroughly confused. Why couldn't he pick one personality and stick with it. Why did he have to change all the time?

"If I could take it all back, but you still knew what I did, would you accept me or reject me?"

"I don't know," I trailed off, picking up another marshmallow. "I'd probably still be your friend. But you can't take everything back. That part of our lives is over."

"Could we start a new friendship?"

I glanced at him. He was again looking into the fire pit, watching the embers dance and glow. I didn't get why he wanted to be friends all of a sudden. It couldn't really be because I went on a date with Ryan. There had to be more to it than that. "Why do you want to be friends again?" I asked.

He sighed, closing his eyes, and setting his head in his hands. He was silent for a few minutes, and I was beginning to wonder if he was even going to answer me, or just leave me hanging. Finally he opened his mouth to reply. "I haven't had anyone I can really be myself with, or trust since I was thirteen-"

"We were friends till we were fourteen," I interrupted him. He didn't even remember when we stopped being close? I found myself a little upset about that.

"Yeah, but I wasn't a good friend to you. I think our friendship kind of fizzled out when I turned thirteen. I thought I was to cool to be best friends with a girl."

"You weren't," I said with a smile. He smirked and glanced at me. "Just saying." I shrugged.

"Thanks, I appreciate the confidence booster."

"You have your fans for that," I replied.

"Listen, Honeybee, I really do want to put the past behind us. I want to be able to come over and complain about the guys on the team, or my parents, or whatever. I miss having someone who actually cares." He took a deep breath. "I miss my best friend." His words pierced my heart more than his eyes did. He missed his best friend, he missed *me*.

"How do I know you're telling me the truth?" I wondered, playing with the ends of my hair. It was a nervous habit.

"I know it's hard to trust that I won't, but I promise, if you give me a second chance, I won't be a jerk to you. I'll even be sort of nice to Bethany," he offered.

"If we're going to be friends, you have to be nice to the ones I already have," I deadpanned.

"So we can be friends again?" he asked hopefully.

"Friends, not best friends. And there are going to be rules." He nodded for me to continue. "Rule number one is that you can't be so mean to me in public."

"There's a week of school left," he said, digging a stick in the embers. "I think I can handle being sort of nice, course I do enjoy some of our fights." He smirked.

"Rule number two is that you'll talk to me tonight about your daddy issues."

At this he looked up and glared. "No, I don't want to talk about that, I don't have issues."

"If you really want to be my friend again, and be able to complain to me about things, you'll talk to me about your issues." I told him, folding my arms across my chest. "Take it or leave it."

"Fine," he said begrudgingly.

I smiled in victory. "I'll start you out with only a few rules, so this is the last one I have for now."

"I bet it's gonna be a massive one."

"You have to let me alter your appearance in two ways for graduation." I beamed.

He scowled at me. "You can't cut my hair or make me wear my socks over my pants. That Halloween still haunts my dreams."

"That may be so, but you were the best nerd ever!" I declared proudly.

He stared at me a few seconds before slowly shaking his head in disgust. "No, I was the worst nerd ever."
"Which makes you the best one," I assured him.

"Your logic is screwed up," he decided, shaking his head.

"My logic is perfectly fine, thank you very much. Now, are you going to take the deal or not? I swear I won't cut your hair or make you wear tube socks. I will let you wear whatever you want," I promised him.

"Pinky promise?" he asked warily, putting his pinky out towards me.

I smirked, locking my pinky around his. "Yes. I pinky promise."

"These things are legit, so no take backs." He released my pinky.

"That would practically be illegal," I said, waving away the idea.

"So we have a deal then, do we not? The rules are set, we've pinky promised. Are we friends again?" his voice dead serious.

"Yes, we're friends," I said, smiling slightly. The friend I thought I'd lost forever was back.

"I think this calls for a hug or something," he decided. A hug? Something was wrong. Maybe he wanted to right his wrongs before he died.

I gulped. "You're worrying me, Lex."

He rolled his eyes and chuckled. "If I was dying, I would tell you. Don't worry, Honeybee."

Did I really ask him if he was dying that often? *Yes.* "How about a handshake to start off with?" I suggested.

"Fine," he shook my hand, then picked up another marshmallow and started to roast it. Suddenly, he dropped it. I raised an eyebrow. Maybe he had burned himself. "I have something for you."

"What?" I murmured. He stood up and walked away. I watched as he dug something out of his bag then came back over and sat down next to me.

"Before you freak out, friends sit next to each other, and I'm not dying," he assured me, a smirk on his lips.

"I wasn't even thinking that," I replied. "What do you have wrapped up under your shirt?" I laughed at the strange shape that was hidden beneath his shirt.

"What I have underneath my shirt will blow your little Honeybee brain!" he declared. "And no, it's not my amazing abs, although, they're pretty stellar,"

"Get to the point," I giggled, nudging him.

"Don't be snappy." He nudged me back. He slowly took the object out from beneath his shirt, producing a brown paper bag, and handed it to me. "Open it."

Inside was a plush pink unicorn. The fabric had faded, and the horn was slightly off. One of the eyes was missing, but the sight of that beaten up unicorn made my heart jump into my throat and tears well in my eyes. It was the unicorn my dad had bought for my first birthday, the one I'd named Garth after Dad's middle name. I'd lost it not long after he died and had been heartbroken for weeks.

"I found him shoved in my closet today when I dug my bag out. I put him in the washing machine so he would smell good when I gave him to you," Lex explained, smiling at my expression of pure joy.

"He does smell good." I couldn't think of what to say, I was so happy my brain couldn't put together the words that I wanted to scream from the rooftops.

"Like lavender, right? Mom gets the good soap." He smirked.

"Thank you." I said, feeling tears fall down my cheeks. "Thank you so much, Lex. You have no idea how much this means to me." I hugged Garth close to me and leaned against Lex.

"You're welcome, Honeybee. It was the least I could do," he returned.

"Sure it was. The least," I replied, rolling my eyes with a laugh. I fought back a yawn.

"That's like the tenth time you've yawned. I think it's time for bed. Don't make me drug you," he threatened.

I smiled, watching the flames dance in front of me. "Fine, but only because we're friends and you found Garth for me, otherwise I would refuse to listen to you." I stood up and started to make my way over to the tent. "Get some sleep, Lex."

"I'll go to sleep soon," he promised. "Sleep well, Honeybee."

"Night, Lex. I'll help you work out your issues tomorrow," I whispered, slipping inside the tent. He laughed quietly at my comment. He probably didn't think I'd be able to help, but I'd prove him wrong.

I crawled into my sleeping bag, holding Garth close to me. The day had turned out to be way better than expected.

The one thing that kept running through my head as my mind drifted off into sleepy land was that Lex and I were *friends*. We were going to be nice to each other. He wasn't going to give away my secrets anymore, and he was going to trust me with his again.

This was going to be so weird.

Chapter Eighteen – Strolling with Stargazer

The sound of someone moving around, outside of the tent Mom and me were sleeping in, woke me up. I thought it was all in my head until I heard another noise. I tensed in my sleeping bag, freaking out internally. Who was outside of my tent? I didn't want to risk waking mom for no reason.

I unzipped my sleeping bag and shivered at the cool night air against my legs. The shorts and long sleeve shirt did little to combat the cool temperatures. I rubbed my arms in an attempt to warm myself up and looked around the dark tent. I couldn't see a thing, not even any light from the moon outside.

After tucking a strand of hair behind my ear, I crept towards where I thought the zipper was. I almost tripped over myself and then reached around until my fingers closed over the small zipper. I slowly pulled it open and peeked out of the small hole.

All of a sudden an eye appeared in front of me. I squeaked and jumped back, falling over my bag and landing hard on my butt. The eye disappeared and two hands slowly pulled the zippers apart to open the tent. I searched around wildly to find something to defend myself, fear coursing through me at a high rate. I grabbed a flip-flop and held it behind me.

Slowly the creeper became visible, but only their outline, it was too dark to see any features. The person started laughing, because apparently they could see me. They held up a light from their phone, and held it near their face. A smile on his face, Lex was laughing at me.

"Lex Diamond! You jerk! I can't believe you just did that!" I hissed, dropping the shoe. "What is wrong with you?"

He laughed, unzipping the tent. "So many things. But since you're up, come with me."

"Lex, it's really late," I told him, even though I had no idea how late it actually was.

His hand went to his side and with it the light of his phone. "Come on."

"It's pitch black outside, and I'm cold. Can't this wait?"

"No! Right now, Bee," he said, sticking his hand out for me to take.

"I don't have shoes," I tried to tell him.

"I'll give you a piggy back ride or something. Now hurry up, who knows how long this will last." He brought his hands together and gave me the puppy dog eyes. I groaned and stepped out of the tent. He grinned and clapped quietly. "Hop on." He turned, crouching down.

"Lex, no," I said, shooing away the idea. "I'll just put my flip-flops on,"

"Olivia Rayne Martin, I will throw you over my shoulder like potatoes," he threatened.

I rolled my eyes, not that he would be able to see it very well. Sighing, I got on his back and he stood up, his arms underneath my knees, and my arms dangling at his chest. I leaned my head on his shoulder, still sleepy. There was a small breeze, and I shivered because of it.

"Cold?" he asked.

I nodded, tightening my hold on him as he walked. "A bit," I agreed.

"This will be worth it," he promised. He kept walking. I could smell the lake on the breeze and assumed that's where we were heading.

"If you're going to kill me and dump my body in the lake, it won't work. Too many people know I came here with you. They all assume we're not friends," I yawned, closing my eyes.

"Don't worry, I won't kill you," he chuckled.

"Thank goodness. Now where are we going?" I asked. He walked along the dirt path, and from the sounds of the crickets and the frogs I could tell we were moving closer towards the lake.

"The lake," he answered.

"I know that. What are we going to see there?" I wondered, a little bit impatient.

"The rest of a meteor shower," he whispered. "I was watching the show at the lake and decided to grab a blanket. When I heard you moving around, I thought you might want to watch it."

"Did you grab the blanket?" I gave a sly grin.

He laughed, his foot catching on a root. I tensed, waiting for him to fall, bringing me with him. Thankfully, he righted himself before we fell. "No, I forgot. I blame you for that."

"Of course." I set my chin on his shoulder and looked towards the lake. "How long have you been watching the meteor shower?" I asked, looking toward the sky. The large trees blocked most of my view, only letting me a few stars sparkling against the black night sky.

"Since after you went to bed," he said, stopping at the lakes shore. "Your seat, my lady," he announced, gesturing to the log. He crouched down so I didn't have to jump off. I sat down on the log and he sat down next to me, staring up at the sky. We watched in silence together as the stars would randomly shoot across the dark night sky. It was like a black canvas, and the artist was throwing streaks of white to entertain the viewers of the painting's creation.

Lex looked enthralled with the sky. His eyes were moving back and forth trying to find the shooting stars. He had his chin in his hand and the faint traces of a smile on his lips. He looked almost innocent, like when we were younger.

"How much do you love the sky?" I asked him.

He took a moment to stop gazing in awe at the stars to look at me. "What kind of question is that?"

I shrugged. "It's a question, now answer it. How much do you love the sky? More than chocolate? More than soccer? How much?" I asked, looking back towards where more stars were shooting around.

"Umm … that's a tough question. Not more than soccer, more than chocolate. It's hard to explain. I just really like watching the stars." He didn't look away from me when he spoke, his eyes still admiring the night.

"Why?" I asked, shivering against the cool breeze coming off the lake. The lake was glowing in the moonlight, and the trees looked eerie in the reflection.

"Why not? The sky is pretty awesome. That might sound really stupid, but it's the truth. The sky is especially awesome at night, or during a storm. Have you ever really paid attention to the sky during a lightning storm, how the lightning travels through the clouds to the ground? It's incredible." The smile lit up his face, and his eyes danced with joy. He looked so happy.

"When did you fall in love with the sky?" He laughed, bringing a frown to my face. Why was that funny?

"I didn't fall in *love* with the sky, Honeybee."

"Just answer the question." I smirked.

Lex smiled and looked out towards the lake, watching the sky in its reflection. "When I was seven or eight, my dad bought me a telescope and put it in my room. That was before his practice took off, so he would spend more time with me watching the stars, searching for planets, or looking for constellations. It was the most fun I ever had with him."

"That's kind of awesome," I whispered, bumping shoulders with him. "I'm guessing that was before you and you dad started to fight more."

He frowned, understanding the direction I was taking. "I guess you could say that."

"Would you?"

"No. I think everything with me changing happened around the same time," he replied, leaning down on his elbows. "High school changed me." He shrugged.

"Do you think you'll ever change back?" I sighed. "At least a little?"

He gave a weak smile. "I hope so."

"Me too," I murmured, leaning against him. He sighed, leaning his head against mine for a moment before he continued to stare at the sky. "How come you never invited me over to watch the stars?"

Grinning, he turned to me. My breath caught in my throat seeing the moonlight in his eyes. *Focus*!

"It wasn't a Honeybee thing. It required too much patience. You wouldn't have lasted an hour," he answered, winking.

I frowned. *I had patience!* "Whatever, I could've."

"Nope, you wouldn't have lasted, trust me. I know you, Bee," he assured me. I rolled my eyes. He didn't know me, not really.

"Can I have your hoodie?" I shivered again. "I'm freezing, and someone forgot to pack my sweat pants." I glared at him.

He looked away innocently. "I'm sorry, what was that?"

"Give me your hoodie or so help me, I'll shove you in the lake," I threatened. Of course, I had no intention of pushing him in the lake. He would retaliate and I would end up worse off than before.

He rolled his eyes, shrugging out of his hoodie and handing it over to me.

"Thank you," I said, pulling it on. I took a deep breath. He smelled good.

"You're welcome. Now be quiet, I want to watch this in peace,"

"But you know I like talking," I protested.

"Then talk to yourself," he laughed.

I scowled at him. *Hmpf.* I *would* talk to myself, just to bug him. "So Olivia, how was your day?" I asked myself. "Oh just great. But I'm curious about water buffalos. Do you think there are any in this lake, being water buffalos and all? I wonder what would happen if a meteorite hit the lake. Would Lex and I die? Or would I live because I ran, rather than watch as the burning rock hit the water's surface. I think I would probably live. I'm way smarter-" A hand clamped over my mouth, and I giggled against it.

"Shush! Honestly, it's like your chatter-box has no off button," he muttered, his hand still on my mouth. I opened my mouth and poked my tongue out. He jumped, and ripped his hand away from me. "Honeybee! You're so gross!"

"You're the one who wanted to be friends again. This is the kind of thing friends' do-"

"And you still won't shut up."

"I just buzz all day long." I winked

He mock gasped. "Did you just make a bee joke about yourself? On purpose?" he wondered.

"No, I never make jokes on purpose." I deadpanned.

"Good to know, Bee," he chuckled.

"You know, it's bad enough you don't even use my real name, but now you're shortening my nickname? I used to have a three syllable nickname, now I'm reduced to one letter. I'm a little offended," I told him.

"I'll stop calling you anything if you keep this complaining up," he mock threatened, glancing back at the sky.

"That's not very nice, taking away a girl's name," I muttered, burying my head in his sweater. Man, why did he smell so good? It was like a mix whatever cologne Lex wore, and the smell of rain after the weather had been dry for a long time.

"Life isn't a fairytale," he chided.

"I've noticed. Which really sucks," I said, sitting back up. "Where's prince charming with a blanket for my freezing legs?"

"How about Prince Lex gives you a piggy ride back to your tent and lets you get some sleep, sound good?" he asked.

"You're a prince?" My eyes widened and my mouth dropped open.

He pushed me slightly. "Get on your feet, peasant. I'm going to give you a ride back to the tent." We stood and he picked me up. His arms were under my knees again. I could feel his muscles pulsing against my skin. Lex stopped at the tent and let me down gently.

"Thanks for letting me in on the meteor shower."

"You're welcome, Bee," he answered, ruffling my hair.

Grumbling, I slapped his arm away. "Hey, don't touch the hair."

"You're not the boss of me," he said, and stuck his tongue out like the mature five year old we both knew he was.

I frowned at him, but it was hard to keep my smile out it. "You're a mean boy." The moon gave his eyes a certain sparkle, like he was thinking of something devious.

"But I'm good at it, right?" he winked. I sighed. He *was* good at it.

"I hope I didn't spoil your time with the sky tonight." The last thing I wanted to do was ruin something special he had with his father.

"No, you didn't, don't worry. It was fun, like old times." He smiled warmly, it reached his eyes.

"Good. Now I'm going to bed. Goodnight, Stargazer," I yawned, unzipping the tent.

"Night, Creeper," he whispered.

"That's creeper crawler to you, I am a honeybee for Pete's sake." I smirked, turning around so I could see him.

"Right, how could I ever forget? Night," he said, winking and heading to his tent.

I watched to make sure he didn't die before he got in his tent. Then I zipped mine all the way up, and got back into my sleeping bag. My eyelids closed and a smile still lingered on my lips.

Chapter Nineteen – Goodbye High School, Hello Summer!

Today was the last day of high school. I was sitting in bed, still smiling at the ceiling. I couldn't believe I was about to graduate from high school, move on to the next part of my life and leave my high school in the dust.

Bethany had planned a last day party at her house for a few of our friends to come over, including Lex, Desmond, Ryan, and his friends. This would be the first time Ryan and Lex would see each other on pleasant terms, since I'd told Ryan about my rekindled friendship. He'd been surprisingly fine with it, I expected more worry.

Ryan and I had gone out again, but we still hadn't talked about whether or not we were officially boyfriend and girlfriend, or if we were just going out to get to know each other better. It was all confusing me greatly, but I didn't know how to ask him about it.

Sighing, I threw back the covers of my bed and the warm California air met me. I got out of bed and quickly got dressed in a pair of white shorts and a bright green V-neck. I slipped on my glasses and threw my hair up in a ponytail. I looked good enough for our last day.

I raced downstairs and grabbed a bowl of cereal. "Morning, Mom." She looked up from her cup of coffee and smiled. "You off to work soon?"

"Yes. Are you ready for your last day as a high schooler?" she wondered, sipping her coffee. Tears shimmered in her eyes. I knew she was holding in her tears for graduation. She thought it was better to cry then, instead of crying a lot beforehand.

"I am completely ready." I glanced at the clock. Lex was giving me a ride since Bethany had to be at the school early for a final project. Today after school, I was going to tell him what two things he had to change about his appearance for the graduation.

Lex had been pretty good about being nice to me at school. The only time he'd really slipped up was during homeroom on Tuesday, but it was obvious he felt guilty about it. He'd apologized and bought me a smoothie after school.

"I still can't believe the past eighteen years have gone by so fast," she murmured, shaking her head. I was about to reply when the door opened. I turned and lifted my head in greeting when Lex walked in.

"Hey." He smiled, glancing over at Mom. "Morning."

"Good morning, Lex." She set her cup down on the counter. "You ready to be done?"

He laughed, nodding his head. "Heck yeah. I've been ready for the past three years."

"I guess that makes sense," Mom agreed.

I moved backward when Lex made a grab for my cereal. "No!" I slapped his hand.

"Debby! Honeybee is being mean to me. Can you punish her please?" he asked, widening his eyes to try and look more innocent. I laughed and pushed him with my shoulder. He barely budged, stupid muscles. "And now she's trying to hurt me," he whined.

"Olivia, be nice to poor Lexie," Mom said, winking at Lex.

He scrunched up his nose. "I thought we talked about this," he started. "When a man turns eight, calling him 'Lexie', is no longer right."

"When you ask me for help, you revert to that little seven year old boy who Olivia had no trouble picking on," Mom explained, shrugging her shoulders. "You want to be treated like a man, don't come crying to mommy when she gets a little rough." She winked, picking up her mug and putting it in the sink. "I'm off to work. Have a good day, and I'll see you later." She hugged us both and left.

"You ready to go?" Lex inquired, a smile tugging at the corners of his mouth.

"Yes, let's go."

Together, we walked to his car and headed to school. On the way, we could see other kids from school, dancing to music in their cars as they drove to their last day of school before the summer.

The sun shone down on the world, the trees sparkling with morning dew, lighting up like a display. It was like the whole universe was happy for the kids at Riverside High. We pulled into the back parking lot and then walked toward the front of the school where most of the students were waiting for class to start.

"I've gotta meet up with the guys to talk about the end of school tradition," Lex informed me, adjusting the bag on his shoulder. "I'll meet up with you later." He waved and walked off.

"See you later."

I found Bethany at one of the tables with a group of students from one of her classes. She had a huge smile on her face. "Can you believe it? Last day!"

"I literally can't!" I shook my head. "But I'm so glad it is!" When someone yelled my name, I turned to see Desmond running over.

"Olivia! Olivia's friend!" he yelled.

Bethany frowned. "I have a name you know," she grumbled annoyed, rolling her eyes. He skidded to a stop next to us.

"Hey," I laughed, giving a small wave.

"Hi!" He glanced at Bethany. "I don't know your name, or I would use it."

"Bethany," she told him.

"Right." He shrugged. "Sorry. Anyways, I need to know where you live so I can come to the party tonight," he said, smiling slightly.

"Why you're invited, I don't know." She sighed. "I'll give the directions to you at lunch, okay? And if all else fails, Olivia will get detention again and explain to you in great detail where I live."

"Okay, great." He was jittery, tapping his fingers against his legs with silent rhythm. "I'm stoked for school to be over."

"We all are." I laughed, continuing to walk towards the schools front doors. Desmond started walking with us. I pulled open the door and walked into the school.

"Are you guys planning to go to any of the parties?" he asked. Bethany and I exchanged glances. We weren't really one for parties.

"I wouldn't count on it," I told him.

"Oh come on. You won't even come to my party? We're friends now. You should come to my parties," he stated, crossing his arms over his chest. What was it with guys throwing tantrums lately?

"Well, we're not really party people." I shrugged. We walked past the crowd of people, moving up the stairs.

"Hot people are party people, and you two are definitely hot," he replied, getting the looks of the people around us. Bethany rolled her eyes.

I laughed. I liked Desmond, he wasn't afraid to be himself. "Thanks, but I'm not going to promise anything."

"Please?" he asked, pushing one of the jocks out of his way as he walked with us. He wasn't even in any of our classes, why was he following us? "Come on, my party is next Saturday, nine to whenever. You can show up and hang out for a little while. Please, it'll make me feel better."

Bethany shook her head. "No. I am going to be gone next weekend. My parents and I are going to D.C., part of my graduation gift."

Desmond scrunched up his eyebrows. "I hope my parents get me something better," he muttered. Bethany glared at him. He put his hands up defensively. "No offense, it's just that seems like no fun to me."

"That's why you aren't going," she retorted, parting ways with me. "I'm off, see you at lunch."

Desmond kept walking with me, but the constant glancing at his watch made it obvious he was running low on free time to socialize. "I'm gonna be late to math if I keep trying to convince you. Promise you'll think about it?" he asked.

I stopped and turned to look at him, raising an eyebrow. "Why do you want me to come so bad?"

"You invited me to a party, so I'm simply returning the favor. Plus we're friends, and good friends don't let friends sit home on a Saturday all by themselves. Think about it?" he questioned again, a smile on his lips.

"Fine, I'll think about it," I relented. "Now go!" I ordered, turning to get to my own class before I did get detention again.

When the final bell rang, signifying it was officially summer, things went crazy. I covered my ears and laughed as the kids around me screamed, laughed, hugged, cried, and ran around like chickens with their heads cut off.

I saw Lex and Desmond running around being crazy with the rest of their teammates. The soccer team had a tradition of making celebratory banners and running around without shirts on, acting like maniacs. They made the cheerleaders look depressed when it came to peppiness.

The football team had a different way of celebrating. They were throwing the ball around randomly when they saw a fellow teammate. It was more dangerous, and less entertaining, which was why I preferred the soccer teams antics.

Bethany came and found me in the craziness and we hugged and laughed, so excited that we were done with it all. The drama, the boys, the crazy girls, the creepers, the teachers, the boring lectures; we were done with the drama of high school. *Finally*!

"We're done!" She smiled, returning her gaze to me.

"I can't believe it!" I exclaimed, my cheeks hurt from smiling so much.

"Believe it, because I'm not sticking around here anymore! We graduate tomorrow, and then, we're done forever! We'll never have to go back to high school." She smiled spinning around in a small circle. I laughed and looked around again. Desmond was still raging on, his shirt on his head and his banner flying about as he ran. The banner simply read '*Done!*'

Lex came running over towards us. His banner read the same thing as Desmond's, except it had a smiley face on it. He had his shirt on his head also, giving every girl he ran past a good view of his abs, no doubt the soccer players did this as a way to show off as well. I tried not to stare, but he did have nice abs, and they were glistening.

"Honeybee!" He yelled above the noise. I jolted, my eyes going to his face instead of his abs. A smirk pulled at the edges of his lips, knowing where my eyes had been moments before. "I'm going to be ready to go in about ten minutes. Will you be ready by then?" he leaned closer so he could hear my reply better.

"Yes!" I beamed.

"Cool. I'm going to finish up with the guys, and I'll be ready to go." He raced away, leaving me staring after him. A pair of fingers snapped in front of my face.

"They're just abs, don't let them suck you in," Bethany laughed, pushing me.

I frowned, but it turned into a smile. "I'll make sure he has his shirt on before he gets in the car," I promised. "I'll see you tonight?" I asked.

"Yes ma'am." She nodded, slipping sunglasses over her eyes. "Besides, if you don't come and Sir Abs does show up, I'm sending everyone to your house," she warned.

"I'll be there," I promised, giving her a hug.

"See you then." She waved and we parted ways.

I made it to the back of the school and walked over towards Lex's car. I only waited a few minutes for him to appear from the back entrance. He still had his shirt off, and his banner was dragging on the pavement behind him. He stopped when he got to the car.

"Thanks for waiting," he said, dropping the banner and getting down on his knees to fold it up.

"Not like I had a choice. I could either wait for you to show up, or wait for the crazy people to finally leave. This seemed like the faster choice." I told him. I watched as he finished folding the banner and put it in the back of his car. "Your shirt is still on your head," I reminded him. He smirked and took it off of his head. His hair messed up slightly because of it.

"Thanks, Captain Obvious." He laughed, pulling his bright blue shirt back on. He pulled his keys out of his gray plaid shorts and unlocked the car. After the car started he headed out. He glanced at me a moment before returning his eyes to the road. "So, about tomorrow, what are you going to make me do?"

I smiled, clapping my hands giddily. I'd been thinking about it a lot. "Well, I think you're really going to love me for what I chose to do to you."
"Oh really? And why is that?"

"Well, they're pretty simple things, and they don't last long," I told him, watching the yellow lines on the road run by. "Are you ready to hear your fate?" He nodded, not taking his eyes away from the road. "Okay, the first thing, is that you have to wear your fire truck red glasses." I told him, watching his reaction.

He didn't freak out like I'd been expecting. "That's no big deal. They're cool, in a retro kind of way. What's the next thing I have to do?" he turned onto our street.

"Well, you're actually coming over to my house to do it tonight," I told him.

He stopped at a stop sign and looked straight at me. "Please explain what you mean before I get the wrong idea."

I blushed, embarrassed by what he might've thought. "I've got some blue hair dye. We're going to give you some streaks."

He frowned and started the car moving again. "I don't really like the idea of that."

"It fades away after a few washes, so it's not going to last very long. We can do this now, or later. Which do you prefer?" I questioned, twiddling my thumbs.

He sighed, pulling into his driveway. "Let's do it now, get it over with. That way, the chlorine will wash some of it out, and–"

"No swimming if you're only doing it to wash it out," I scolded, shaking my head.

"Fine, I won't go swimming, but I will take my shirt off. You can't stop me from doing that!" he declared getting out of the car.

"I noticed," I replied, hopping out of the car. I grabbed my bag and looked at him across the hood.

"I saw you noticing." He smirked, a twinkle in his dark irises.

Blushing, I ignored him and turned away. "I'll get everything set up. Come over in about ten minutes wearing clothes you won't mind getting blue."

With a wave, I walked across the street quickly and went inside. My cheeks were flaming and I leaned against the door.

Curse his ability to make me blush.

Chapter Twenty – The Smurf

Lex came over dressed in basketball shorts and a black muscle shirt. I wore a big white t-shirt and some old jean shorts. My hair swayed in a ponytail as I moved out of the way to let him in.

Mom was leaning against the banister at the top of the stairs. "Livie told me all about her plot." She smiled, "If you need any help, just holler." She disappeared down the hall to her room.

Lex followed me upstairs and into the bathroom. I had a chair all set up and everything. "Your throne," I said, bowing sarcastically. He laughed and sat down. Since he was tall, sitting down his head was at my chest, so I could easily reach it and put blue dye in it. I was probably more excited than I should've been.

"I'm at your mercy," he said meekly.

I smirked. "Yeah, you are." After putting the gloves on, I grabbed the bottle of dye, and turned to see his face staring at me in the mirrors reflection. He looked nervous. I held back a laugh.

"Be gentle," he pleaded.

I started to dye his hair, taking pieces of foil and folding strips of his hair into them after I'd plastered it with blue dye. The longer I stared at the amount of foil in his hair, the more I realized that there was undoubtedly a lot of *blue* in his hair as well. I bit my lip.

"Bee, please tell me you didn't make some huge mistake and dye my hair with permanent blue dye, or something worse," he murmured, apparently having seen my look of concern in the reflection.

"What? No, of course not," I scoffed, feigning confidence. I set the bottle down and looked at him. "We have to leave it in for a little while longer for the blue to really set." I bit my lip again, surveying the nearly empty dye bottle. I'd used too much. Nodding to myself, I accepted that this would be my last day on earth.

"The fact you're freaking out more than I am makes me nervous," he noted, raising an eyebrow as he looked at his reflection. I didn't say anything, just excused myself to get away to my room for a few moments before he killed me.

When the blue had been in long enough, I turned him away from the mirror so he wouldn't see his reflection, and started pulling the foil out. There was so much blue. I was seriously starting to worry for my life.

With all of the foil out, I moved him to the shower and turned on the water to start washing all the excess out. Blue spilled from his head, pooling in the bottom of the shower below, circling the drain.

"That is a lot of blue," his voice sounded nasally since his head was upside down.

"That means there's less in your hair." I hoped I was right.

When there wasn't any blue was coming out of his hair, I gave him a towel and he dried his hair out. I made him close his eyes and turn around in a way so that he couldn't see the mirror. "Okay, take the towel off." I instructed.

"Can I open my eyes, too?" he laughed.

"Yes, you can." I replied. He opened his eyes and took the towel off. I crossed my arms, one arm against my chest, and I tapped my chin, surveying my work. *Yep.* He would probably kill me. There was way more blue than I expected.

"You look scared," he said, pulling his eyebrows together. "How bad is it?" he asked.

I shrugged. "Define bad..."

He turned around and looked in the mirror. His eyes widened and his jaw dropped. I had told him I would give him a few streaks. I was pretty sure what I'd done was more along the lines of highlights, lowlights, and streaks. There was almost more blue than there was blond.

"This is catastrophic." He ran a hand through the blue mess. He turned to me and pointed a finger. "This is going to be horrible for pictures tomorrow," he worried, looking back at his reflection.

I cringed. I hadn't thought about pictures. "Lex, I'm so sorry, I didn't know it would turn out like this." I covered my face with my hands.

"How many washes does it last through?"

"Umm, I think it said ten washes," I whimpered. I had ruined his graduation. I was a horrible human being, and I would never be a hairstylist. That much was for sure.

"I'm going to go home and wash my hair a ton, and then I'm going swimming tonight. Hopefully, there will be less blue by tomorrow," he murmured, pulling at some of the blue hair.

"Lex, I'm so sorry!" I cried, feeling horrible.

He scratched his head awkwardly, like he wasn't sure how to react. He walked over to where I was and wrapped his arms around me. I stiffened. Lex Diamond was giving me a hug? The earth was off its axis or something.

"It's alright. One day we'll look back at this and laugh. But, for now, I'm going to go try and get the blue to fade." He let me go and surveyed himself in the mirror once again.

"We can ask my mom," I said, feeling so very helpless.

He shook his head quickly. "The fewer people who see it, the better."

"Can I take a picture?" I inquired, biting my lip. "That way if I ever think about dying my own hair, or someone else's, I'll know better."

"Yeah, I guess that's okay," he snickered. I ran from the bathroom and went to grab my camera.

"How goes the dying?" Mom asked from her room.

I skidded to a stop and froze. "Lex doesn't really want people to see."

"Well now I have to go see it," she deadpanned, heading towards the bathroom. At least we'd have someone to take the picture for us. I got back in the bathroom and Lex was sitting against the counter.

Mom was staring at him, mouth agape. "It's just so … blue," she breathed, dumbfounded.

I handed her the camera and went to stand next to him. "Take our picture?"

She turned on the camera and took a few pictures. "I will never let her near your hair again. I should've known better. Sorry, honey," she said to Lex.

"It's okay." He slid an arm around my waist, sending shivers up my back. Mom took a few pictures. "It was a good growing experience for her and me. I won't ever let an inexperienced person touch my hair again," he swore.

Letting go of my waist, he stood. "I'll be back in a little while. Be ready to go."

"I will," I answered. He left.

Mom turned to me. "Well, thank goodness you didn't choose to do that bright pink color. That would've been horrific." She kissed my forehead and left me alone. I stared at the mirror. I had possibly just ruined Lex's graduation day, and yet, he didn't try to kill me.

Maybe Lex *was* changing.

Lex came back around 6:45 P.M. He was wearing the same shirt, but his shorts were hot pink with black zebra stripe. I raised my eyebrows.

"It's a soccer thing," he supplied with a shrug.

"Oh, okay." *Because that makes sense.* I was still wearing the big tee shirt; it covered my bathing suit pretty well. I looked at his hair and immediately felt depressed when I saw that it was still super blue.

He noticed where my eyes went. "It didn't work as well as I'd hoped. Hopefully though, Bethany's pool will work better than shampoo." He gestured towards the car. "Shall we go?"

"Yeah, let's go. Bethany said she'd send everyone to my house if I wasn't there," I told him, walking towards the car. He laughed, opening my door for me. "Thanks." I smiled as I got in.

"Bridges never ceases to amuse me with her threats." He grinned, shutting my door and heading to his side. "I think it's a gift," I murmured.

"Perhaps." He pulled away from the curb, heading towards Bethany's.

"Is Cassy coming tonight?" I glanced over at him. The setting sun cascaded through the windshield, casting a golden hue onto his already tan skin. The blue in his hair gleamed, contrasting with skin.

He shook his head. "No, she had plans already. I'm flying solo tonight."

A few minutes down the road I again looked at his blue hair. I still felt like the worst person ever. What kind of monster ruined someone's hair the day before graduation?

"Don't freak out, Bee." He smirked, seeing me in the corner of his eye.

I frowned, crossing my arms over my chest. "I turned your head blue. You could pass for a Smurf, for crying out loud! I should freak out a little bit."

He glanced in the rearview mirror, watching the group of kids behind him. They were riding their bikes down the sidewalk. "That was more of an insult than an apology." He paused, waiting for the kids to pedal past him before he turned onto Bethany's street.

"Sorry," I said again, putting my head in my hands.

"It's not as bad as it looks. My mom saw it and thought I was going for a patriotic look," he told me. Lex parked along the curb and turned the car off. He turned to me. "I'm not mad. I said you could do it. Granted, I didn't know how it would turn out, but I should've known better." He smirked as I frowned. "Now let's go inside okay? I've got to get some good swimming in if I want to try and lighten the color more." He looked at his hair again.

"It does look more faded since this afternoon," I said, trying to sound positive.

"It's dry too, instead of just towel dried. So that helps. I'll just have to make it work tomorrow. I'll shove it all under my hat or something," he winked, getting out of the car.

I got out to and grabbed my bag. He locked his car and we started towards the front door. We could hear everyone else in the backyard laughing and talking. I led him over to the door leading to the backyard and walked in.

"Olivia!" Desmond yelled loudly, getting the attention of everyone inside.

"Desmond is here?" Lex complained from behind me.

"Yes, he is. And you two are going to pretend that you're best friends," I replied.

Ryan and all of his friends were there. Desmond, Ryan, Billy, and Rick were playing something in the pool, probably Marko-Polo. Bethany, Noelle, and Grace were all in chairs laughing and talking. I wondered where Grace's boyfriend Aaron was.

Lex looked out of place, standing there almost awkwardly, mainly because when everyone looked at him, they saw his blue head. Noticing the stares, Lex seemed to straighten, standing taller. I let a small smile slip at his confidence.

"Dude, what the heck happened to your hair?" Desmond inquired, wiping the water from his eyes.

"Consider it a graduation gift that overdosed," Lex said flippantly, walking past the guys and over to a chair where he sat down.

"Olivia, are you going to get in?" Ryan swam over to the edge.

I bent down, sitting on my knees. "I need to put my stuff down and say hi to the girls, but then I'll get in," I promised.

"Good, but hurry up. I wanna dunk you." He smiled giddily.

"Sounds great." I remarked sarcastically. He stretched up, kissing my cheek before returning to the other guys. I stood up and walked over to where the girls, and Lex, were all sitting.

Bethany stood up and gave me a hug. "You're so spilling later what happened to Lex's hair."

I laughed and walked over to the other girls and smiled. "Hey guys," I said, giving a general wave.

"Hey Livie, long time no see!" Noelle smiled. She was wearing a bright pink bikini, a belly button ring sparkling in the fading sunlight.

"Yeah, forever almost," I jested, glancing at Grace who smiled at me. Her dark brown hair was in a braid, and she was wearing a grey one piece bathing suit with shorts. "Hey Grace," I smiled. "Where's Aaron?"

"He had work tonight, sadly," she replied.

"Lame," I said and set my stuff down on one of the chairs and slipped my flip-flops off. I lifted my shirt over my head and dumped it with my stuff. I then let my hair fall down from the pony tail.

"Okay, I'm going to go get dunked," I said, glancing back at Ryan who had Billy in a headlock.

"Have fun," Noelle called with a laugh. I walked over to the edge of the pool and saw it glimmer under the sun.

"I hope Honeybees can swim!" Lex called right before he pushed me in. I screamed and barely managed to hold my breath before I hit the water. The chill of the water sent shivers down my spine. I rubbed my arms under the water before pushing off the bottom of the pool and surfacing.

As I broke the surface, I saw that Lex was still standing there, smirking like he was king of the pool or something. I frowned and splashed him before swimming toward where Ryan was. Ryan met me half way and smiled.

"Hey," I said, smiling. He glanced at Lex who had moved back to his chair. He had his sunglasses on over his eyes, and he was looking at his phone. He was probably bored already. "How was the ride over?"

"It was fine. I told you, we're friends again. It's okay." I promised.

"If you say so," he said. I took a minute to take in Ryan's appearance. He had on black board shorts, and the water came just a bit below his chest. He too had well defined abs, I would make sure to get in a good hug before he put his abs away. He winked, catching me staring. I bit my lip, feeling the heat spread across my cheeks. Laughing, Ryan looked back at Lex. "Are you going to come swimming?" he called out. "Unless you'd rather gab with the girls," Ryan taunted.

Lex lifted his head, looking our way. Encouraged by the taunt, Lex took his sunglasses off and then his shirt. The butterflies stirred when his abs were on display again. He walked over to the edge, slipping into the pool. "Happy now?" he raised an eyebrow.

"I suppose. Are you?" Ryan wondered, raising an eyebrow as well. It was like some kind of gentle standoff.

"He better be," Desmond mumbled, swimming over. Billy and Rick swam over as well. I looked up when the other girls got into the water. Noelle slid next to Rick, and his arms encircled her waist.

Ryan looked from his friends to Lex. "Do you know everyone?"

Lex glanced at the group of strangers, shaking his head. "Never met them. I'm Lex Diamond," he introduced himself, nodding at each of them.

"This is Billy, and Rick." Ryan gestured to them as he said their name. "That is Noelle and Grace." The girls smiled.

"Nice to meet you guys," Lex murmured, shooting a glance my way as if to make sure I saw him being polite to the guys. I gave a smile in reply.

"I take it you know Desmond already?" Billy mentioned, tipping his head toward where Desmond was standing.

Lex grimaced. "Yeah." I cleared my throat. "We're on the same soccer team, and apparently we're best friends."

"Wait, what?" Desmond gaped, glaring at Lex. "When did this happen?"

Lex jerked a thumb in my direction. "Honeybee's declared that we're to act civil and pretend we're best friends. Don't blame me." I grinned, shaking my head.

"Seriously?" Desmond moped, his head drooping. "You know we can't stand each other, right?"

"I do, but I also know that if I'm going to be friends with both of you, you're going to see each other on occasion. I'd rather it wasn't a blood bath each time you set eyes on each other," I admitted. "Plus! You can both be

mad at me for it, and it'll be a bonding experience."
Desmond and Lex glared at each other, apparently not
liking the idea.

"Tag anyone?" Billy suggested, trying to break the
tension.

Ryan grinned at me. "Olivia's it."

It was like something exploded, shooting each of them
away from me simultaneously. Sighing, I bolted toward
whoever was closest to me.

For the next half an hour we played tag, splashing and
swimming as fast as we could to avoid being tagged. I was
hit a few times, mostly by Lex and Ryan. Desmond and
Lex made it their mission to tag each other as hard as
possible, leaving red marks. Bethany left and went inside to
help her mom finish getting things ready for when we all
went inside for food and movies.

Desmond charged past me in the water, Lex right
behind him. Unable to stop himself, he ran right into me,
dunking me under the water. His hands found my waist,
pulling me back up from the water. "You okay?"

I sputtered, nodding as I coughed up water. "Yup."

"Good, cause you're it." He smirked. "No tag backs." I
glared and was about to protest when Bethany came back
outside, standing on the deck.

She had her hands on her hips. "If you all want to
come inside, there is a food and a movie." She glanced over
at Noelle and Rick who were pulling themselves from the
water. "And everyone dry off a bit before you come in, or
my mom will kill you with a butter knife," she mentioned.
"And that'll be a slow death."

"I'm afraid," Desmond deadpanned, glancing at me.

"Alright," Billy called, shoving Ryan back down into the water before he hauled himself out of the water.

Lex sighed, standing next to me. "And I just tagged you."

I smirked, shaking my head and swam to the edge. Moving to my chair, I wrapped up in my towel to dry off. The rest of the girls had already gone inside. I looked to see the guys all out and drying themselves off. Pulling my shirt back on, and twisting my hair into a bun, I headed inside.

The countertops sparkled under the lamp hanging from the idle of the ceiling, and the wooden floor was cold from the A.C. I shivered slightly and quickly went to grab some food. We girls had to get our food before the guys came in and made the food disappear with their magical stomachs that never filled up.

"Mom made hotdogs and hamburgers, and we have chips and sliced up fruit. I'm going to go set up the movie," Bethany said, and left the room.

We all started serving up our food and we were walking into the living room to sit down when the guys made their way in. Desmond and Lex still had their shirts off, what their reason for that was, I had no clue.

I sat down on the couch next to Noelle and Bethany, Grace on the other side of Noelle. There was a table in front of us for our drinks to be set on. The other two sofas were smaller, but there would be enough room for the guys.

"What movie did you pick?" Rick asked, coming and sitting down in the green couch across from us.

"That's a surprise! I've got it all set up, so I don't even have to go to the main menu." Bethany smiled.

I rolled my eyes and took a bite of my hotdog. "She enjoys making people guess. It's her little game," I told him, sipping some water.

"Grace does the same thing. Whenever I ask her what we're watching she makes me try and guess. It's so annoying!" Billy groaned as he came into the living room. He surveyed the seating arrangement and took the spot on the empty couch. "I'm a lone wolf," he supplied when we looked at him.

"Is it a Disney movie?" Desmond asked, taking the spot next to Billy.

Billy sighed. "There goes my lone wolf-ness."

Desmond elbowed him. "Dude, you don't want to talk like that. No wonder you don't have a girlfriend." Grace gave a small laugh, which caused Billy to glare in her direction. She stopped laughing and looked away from him.

Ryan walked in, with a plate in his hands. "Billy's a stud." He took the spot next to Rick. Next to come in was Lex, who sat down next to Desmond.

"Have you guys figured out what the movie is yet?" Ryan glanced at Bethany.

"Nope," she answered. "They haven't even bothered to make any guesses." Of course as soon as the Bond music came on, everyone knew exactly what she'd put into watch.

"I love this movie," Desmond said, "There are hot chicks in it." I rolled my eyes.

"Is that all you ever think about?" Lex wondered.

Desmond glared at him. "Best friends, remember? We support each other."

Lex snorted, nodding his head. "Yes, of course. Apologies."

"Friends sometimes, am I right?" Desmond grinned, slapping Billy's shoulder. I settled in against the couch to watch the movie and enjoy my last night as a high school senior.

Around nine o'clock Rick and Noelle headed home, soon after Grace and Billy left as well. By nine thirty, Ryan was leaving too. After he said goodnight to Desmond, Lex, and Bethany, I went outside with him to say goodnight.

He hugged me and kissed my cheek. "I guess I'll see you later then, have fun graduating tomorrow, okay?"

I nodded, leaning my head against his chest. "As soon as it's over I'm going to be the happiest girl ever." I let go and looked up at him.

"Good." His ring glinted in the faint light as he twisted it with his tongue. It was a habit of his.

"Can I ask you something?" I murmured, biting my lip nervously.

"Of course," he replied, brushing my bangs from my eyes. "Anything."

I took a deep breath, trying to steady my heartbeat. "What … are we? We've gone on a few dates. We hang out a lot and flirt. But I don't know what to call you."

The smile on his lips weakened. "I'm not sure. What do you want to be?"

A frown fell to my lips when I realized he'd put the ball back in my court. "I don't know. I've never been in a relationship before, and I don't know when to classify something as such." He smiled. "So I don't know if I should consider us to be a couple if we've only gone on a few dates. I mean, how do you know when it's serious and when it's just for fun?"

He chuckled, shrugging his shoulders. "I don't really know. But I think the easiest way to decide what this is, is to figure out if we have real feelings for each other, or we just enjoy each other's company in the friendly sense."

I'd only ever had real feelings for Lex, and I wasn't sure what feelings for Ryan felt like. Sure, I liked him, and I thought he was cute. But I wasn't the kind of person to take dating casually. I had to feel like there was a possible future before I let someone call me their girlfriend. Biting my lip, I met his eyes and shrugged. I didn't know how I felt about him.

Ryan sighed, rubbing the back of his neck. "After getting to know each other these past few weeks, if you don't know what your feelings are toward me, I think that's an answer all in itself."

"I'm sorry, Ryan," I mumbled, looking away from him. Why couldn't I fall for him? He was wonderful.

"It's okay. Can't win them all," he murmured. "I knew coming into it that you were in love with someone else."

"Still," I muttered, mad with myself. "You're a great guy. I'm stupid for not falling in love with you."

He laughed. "As great as I am, I can't make all the ladies fall for me." I sighed. "But hey, at least I've gained another friend out of this."

"Yes." I met his gaze. "You most definitely did." Reaching up, I wrapped my arms around his neck, feelings his slide around my waist. "There is a very lucky girl out there somewhere."

He pulled away. "And there is a lucky guy sitting on that couch inside." His eyes dimmed. "I just hope he realizes it before it's too late."

"Me too," I whispered, feeling an ache in my chest.

"Goodnight, Olivia," he murmured, walking backwards toward his car.

"Night, Ryan." I watched him get into his car and he waved before driving off.

When I walked back inside Desmond and Lex were helping Bethany clean up. Bethany laughed at something Desmond said, hair falling over her shoulders. Desmond flashed a flirtatious grin, winking as she walked away.

Lex looked like he wanted to hit Desmond, but clenched his fists at his sides. When he saw me, his body relaxed. "Thank goodness. I need to leave before I have to hurt my *best friend*."

"I'm a little offended by that," Desmond shot back, leaving the kitchen.

"Sorry," Lex muttered sarcastically. Desmond glared, starting over toward Lex.

Bethany came to the rescue. "You guys should get going. We all have a big day tomorrow, wouldn't want to scar any faces before then."

"Fine," Desmond grumbled, grabbing his shirt and pulling it on. Lex had long since put his shirt back on.

Laughing, Bethany gave me a hug goodbye. "I still want to hear all about the graduation gift you gave Lex," she smirked.

"What is there to tell? All the information you need is right here on my head. Bright and blue as ever," Lex sighed, his eyes glaring at the blue hair that touched his eyebrows.

"It seems to have faded some," she told him as we all walked outside, the cool night air making me shiver. I hadn't realized it was that cold when I'd said goodbye to Ryan.

Lex paused beside her. "Bridges that may very well be the nicest thing you've ever said to me."

"Don't get used to it." She waved goodnight to Desmond.

"Night all!' he called, waving as he got into his car and sped off.

"Bye," I called, as Lex and I walked over to his car.

The ride was quiet, the cool summer breeze blowing past us and making the night seem so peaceful. We got to his house in a matter of minutes. He parked and turned off the car. We both got out of the car and I started to walk over towards my house.

"Night, Honeybee," he called. I turned and smiled.

"Goodnight, Lex. Sleep well."

"You too," he returned.

I got inside and locked the door, heading up to my room. I changed quickly from my bathing suit into my pajamas and crawled under my sheets, exhausted. I hugged Garth to my chest.

T-minus one day until I was officially graduated.

Chapter Twenty One – It's Graduation, Baby!

My heart was filled with joy as I watched the lights drop and the principal step up to the microphone. Shuffling feet echoed lightly when the first row of graduates moved toward the stage.

"It is my honor to be here with you all today," Principal Bitsley boomed, looking over the crowd. The light gray suit he wore was snug over his portly stomach. He wore a crown of salt and pepper hair, his bald spot almost blinding in the spotlight. "This class has worked hard for four years to be here today, and it is my privilege to hand them the diplomas they deserve." He smiled, picked up the first diploma, and began reading names off the list.

I waited anxiously in my seat, watching as he congratulated student after student. Since my last name started with M it would be a little ways before it was actually my turn. Even Bethany would have a while to wait with the huge class graduating with us.

As each of my friends crossed the stage to accept their diplomas, I cheered loudly. Bethany accepted her humbly, offering sincere gratitude and a smile. Desmond was cocky, winking and waving at the crowd as he sauntered over. Lex was confident, head held high, and shoulders back. He'd styled his hair in a faux-hawk, concealing a lot of the blue under his cap, and he wore his red glasses proudly.

After what seemed like forever, my name was finally called. Everything seemed to move in slow motion. Lights flashed slowly, delayed. Mom's cheering seemed to be weak, slowly building to a louder volume.

My knees shook as I walked across the stage, a bright light shining down on me. Flashes went off in the crowd, but I kept my eyes focused on the piece of paper in Principal Bitsley's hand. Sweat trickled down my neck.

"Congratulations, Olivia," his words were muddled together as I accepted the paper, vaguely aware of the screams of excitement around me. My feet carried me off stage as the next student crossed the stage.

Before I knew it, all the students had crossed the stage, and Principal Bitsley announced our graduated class. Chaos broke out as all the students threw their hats into the air, screams mingling with laughter.

In a rush, caps and gowns were discarded on chairs while everyone separated to find family and friends. I pulled off my gown, revealing the short charcoal colored dress. It hit just above my knees, and had a sweetheart neckline.

Pushing through the crowd, I reached the row where Mom and Diamond's were. Lex was standing by his Mom, her arm around his waist, tears staining her cheeks. Lex had also shed the stuffy black gown, revealing his dark gray slacks and white dress shirt with sleeves rolled up to his elbows. The top button was undone, revealing tan skin, and his tie was hanging, undone, against his chest.

He met my eyes as I walked over, a smile twinkling in their depths. "Honeybee." He left his mother's side and walked over to me, wrapping his arms around me tightly. I hugged him back. His breath tickled my neck as he leaned down. "Congrats!"

I leaned back, his arms still locked around me. "Thanks, Lex. I'm surprised you made it this far," I jested.

He laughed, releasing me and shaking his head. "Sometimes you're so hurtful, Honeybee."

"I learned from the best," I retorted, moving toward Mom. She had tears in her eyes and when she hugged me, I could feel her shaking as they fell down her face.

"I'm so proud of you, sweetheart," she cried, standing back, her hands gripping my shoulders. "Your father would be so proud to be here today."

I bit the inside of my cheek to distract my already frazzled emotions. I'd spent two hours that morning crying because Dad wasn't going to be there to see me walk across the stage, or hug me afterward and tell me how proud he was. "Thanks, Mom."

A hand clasped around my shoulder, as Bethany appeared beside me. I turned and hugged her, laughing. "Can you believe it?" she squealed.

"I thought I was going to faint when I crossed the stage!" I cried, laughing with her. Behind her, Desmond appeared, joining the hug. Lex stood by, hands in his pockets. "Desmond!"

"I'm so glad to be done!" he let go and we all stepped back. "No more high school. I've been looking forward to this since junior year."

I laughed. "I've been looking forward to it since freshmen year, so I think I win." He frowned, nudging my shoulder playfully.

"Bethany!" her mom called, standing at the edge of the row. "Come on, sweetie. Your grandparents have to get home before too long, and they want to take you out." She waved at the rest of us standing there.

Bethany sighed, pushing her hair behind her ear. "Alright, I guess I need to go." She hugged me once more. "We're hanging out before I leave for D.C. though," she decided, looking at Desmond, Lex, and I. Normally, she and I would've spent the night together after a big event like graduation, but she was spending the evening at a hotel with her family.

"Of course," Desmond gasped. "It would be criminal if we didn't." She laughed, waving before she turned to meet up with her family. He turned back to us. "I should probably get going also. See you ladies later." He gave a cheeky grin, sprinting away before Lex could hit him.

"I can't believe you're making me pretend to be best friends with someone so immature," Lex mumbled, rubbing his eyes.

"I think you're matched in maturity," I quipped, smiling brightly before turning back to Mom. She was wiping her eyes. "Mom, are you going to be okay?"

"I'll be alright eventually," she gave a short laugh. "Why don't we follow the direction of everyone else and get some food? I can drown my sorrows in fried foods."

I looped my arm through hers. "At least now I know where I get that trait from."

"I think that is just a girl thing," Patty inserted, placing a hand on my shoulder. "Oh well. Let's go, Mama's gotta drown some sorrows." She pulled Steve with her toward the exit. Mom kissed my cheek, following her lead. Lex and I fell into step beside behind them.

"So where is Cassy?" I wondered, turning to look at him.

He opened in his mouth in question, as his eyes scanned over the crowd. "I don't know. I haven't seen her for a few days."

"Isn't it something couples do? See each other on big days of the year," I trailed off, raising an eyebrow. "How can you not see your girlfriend on graduation day?"

He shrugged. "How can you not see your boyfriend?"

I chose not to correct him. "That's different. We've known each other a few weeks and he has work. You've been dating her since last summer-"

"Off and on," he interrupted, putting a hand on the small of my back as he led me out of the school. I bit back a shiver. "And he can't possibly work all day."

"He might," I argued, a grin on my lips. "Besides, you guys separate for a few hours at best before getting back together. So what happened?"

He chewed on his bottom lip, like he was contemplating whether or not to trust me. "Something did happen," he admitted.

"Are you going to tell me about it?" I prodded, nudging his arm.

He sighed. "It's not exactly exciting material." I nudged him again. "I sort of went over to her house to surprise her. Turns out I'm the one who got to be surprised. She was entertaining another guy."

I cringed, turning my face away. "I'm sorry, Lex."

"Me too." He held the door open, and we walked outside. The cool night air was a relief to my warm skin. Standing in a gym for two hours with two hundred students, plus all the other people in attendance was not fun "But it isn't the first time."

"Why are you still with her if she keeps cheating on you?" I wondered, crossing my arms over my chest.

"To be honest, I'm not sure. I didn't know she was cheating on me at first, and then when I found out..." he shrugged. "I guess it was pride. I didn't want people to know she was cheating on me, so I ignored it."

"Maybe you should get over yourself and stop dating someone who doesn't like you enough to be exclusive," I murmured, biting my lip. Friends were honest with each other, but I wasn't sure how honest he wanted me to be with him.

"Way to bash me," he snickered, turning his head to watch me. "You know, Honeybee, I've underestimated you. You've got more guts than I ever gave you credit for."

I blushed, turning away. "If that's a compliment, I can't tell."

"I think it is," he supplied as we reached the cars where Mom and the Diamond's were waiting for us.

"Slow pokes," Patty chided, her arm tucked under Steve's. "Let's go before all the restaurants are closed or full of graduates."

We ended up picking a burger joint. The booth we sat in was circular, with dark green leather covering the seats. The dark cherry wood table, which was clean when we got to the restaurant, was now littered with plates as we ate and laughed.

"Remember when the kids had a pool party in the bathtub?" Patty questioned, sipping her iced tea. Lex glanced my way, eyebrows raised nervously. He was on one end of the booth, Steve on the other. I was sitting between Lex and mom.

"Oh I remember," Mom muttered. "It took me two days to clean up the mess they made." She shot us both glances, which we avoided.

"It took me a while to clean up the catastrophe that became our garage when they tried to make their own lemonade stand," Steve chuckled, glancing at Lex. Thankfully, Lex had a smile on his face and didn't glare. Maybe things were getting better between them, or he was just in too good of a mood to be mad.

"If that had taken off, we would've made you guys rich," Lex claimed, stealing a French fry from my plate.

"Or something," I agreed, pushing blonde bangs behind my ear. Lex was still sporting his red glasses, and actually seemed to be taking back part of his old personality. He wasn't worried about who would see us together, or what people would think. He was just enjoying himself. My heart swelled with happiness.

"I still remember the excitement on your faces when Max and I built your tree house," Steve murmured, glancing at me. I clenched my jaw, forcing a small smile. "You two were so excited, you couldn't stop jumping, even though it took a little over a month for us to finish it."

"Least we got some good exercise in, right?" Lex jested. Was he trying to lighten the mood I could feel falling over me? It was possible he was that observant, he did know me better than most people.

"Yeah."

"My goodness, remember the first time you two slept in the tree house for the night?" Mom wondered, resting her elbows on the table.

"No."

"Are you kidding?" Patty laughed, but she sounded so far away. "If they don't, I do. I don't think I'd ever been so afraid for them in my life."

"We had it under control," Steve chuckled, kissing Patty's cheek. "You just didn't trust us men to take care of the young ones. I don't know why."

"Yes, because you two were so trustworthy when you were together," Mom's voice was garbled. Lex glanced at me, but I couldn't look back at him. My mind was already falling into that memory.

"Daddy!" I screamed, curling up in a ball against the wall of the tree house, my tree house. It was so pretty. Daddy made sure it was pretty because I was a princess, and I needed a pretty castle. Daddy and I put lots of pictures of butterflies, frogs, and princesses on the walls. Heavy footsteps crossed the deck below, and then the tree swayed lightly as he climbed up. Blond hair appeared at the top of the ladder, a bright smile shining on his face. I instantly felt more relaxed.

"Sweetheart, I'm right here. You don't have to be afraid." Daddy pulled himself into the tree house, and crossed the floor to sit next me. He picked me up and cradled me in his lap. "What happened?" I shrugged, snuggling closer to him. Daddy turned, steel blue eyes narrowing in on Lex who was sitting in the opposite corner. "Lex, do you know what happened?"

Lex shook his head, shaggy blond locks falling into his green eyes. "No, Mr. Martin." I frowned. He did know what happened! Lex shot me a look, fear in his eyes. He was scared of getting in trouble.

Daddy hugged me tighter, his arms acting like a cocoon of safety. "Well, whatever scared you, you don't have to worry about it, Livie. I'll protect you."

I smiled up at Daddy, snuggling closer to him. He smelled like cocoa, probably because I had spilled it on him earlier. But I liked the smell. Maybe I would have to do that more often. "From all the monsters?"

"Of course, sweetie." He kissed the top of my head, settling back against the wall. "So, what were you two up to before you got scared?"

"We were spying on the neighbors," Lex piped up, a toothy grin on his face. He was so lucky. He'd already lost some of his teeth, and the tooth fairy had visited his house. I still hadn't lost one yet. Lex told me I wasn't old enough.

Daddy chuckled, the sound louder in the confined space. "Really? See anything interesting?" he wondered.

Lex slipped out of his sleeping bag, binoculars in hand, and walked over. "There's a new puppy down the street." There were only a few other houses that we could see into from the tree house. One of them belonged to the Avery's, and they were the ones who got a new puppy.

"Really?" Daddy leaned forward, taking the binoculars. "What kind of puppy was it?"

"A really big one!" Lex clapped his hands, settling down next to Daddy. "Dad told me we could have a puppy."

"Are you going to get a big one?" he adjusted the binoculars and looked out the window toward the houses.

"A really, really big one!" Lex nodded, puffing his chest out proudly. "It'll eat all the other dogs." I squealed, hiding my face in Daddy's shirt.

Daddy's arms clasping around me again. "Livie, is that what scared you?"

"I mean-" Lex tried to correct himself before he got in trouble. "It's going to save all the puppies!"

"You're lying!" I shouted, glaring at him. "You said it would eat all the puppies! You're mean!"

"I didn't mean it!" He claimed, jumping to his feet.

Daddy put a hand on Lex's shoulder. "It's okay, buddy." He turned to me. "Olivia, I'm sure Lex didn't mean it like that."

"No!" I shouted again. "He did! He wants to hurt all the puppies!"

"I didn't mean it!" he tried again, clenching his fists tighter. "I swear!"

"Mommy says not to swear!" I screamed, pulling from Daddy's arms and shoving Lex.

He tumbled back, knocking over the little table with our milk and cookies. The milk splashed to the ground, soaking into the bedding. Lex collided with the wall, a small sound escaping his lips as he hit it.

"Olivia!" Daddy scolded, moving over to Lex. "You okay, Lex?"

"I'm fine," he muttered, choking back tears. His face was bright red, and his eyes blazed.

"Everything okay up here?" Mr. Diamond's head appeared in the doorway. He saw the two of us on the floor

and frowned. "I'm gone for five minutes and something bad happens."

Daddy glanced at Mr. Diamond a moment before turning his attention back to Lex. "Are you sure you're alright?" Why was he so concerned for Lex? Shouldn't he be angry? Lex was swearing and wanted his dog to eat all the other puppies! That was bad! Daddy turned back to me, a frown on his face. "Olivia, you don't push your friends."

Milk slid down the wall where it had splashed, and the cookies lay broken on the ground. I frowned. "I'm sorry."

"She's lying!" Lex pouted, crossing his arms over his chest. "She hates me!"

I gasped, tears springing to my eyes. "No I don't!" I fell back against the floor and hid my face against my knees.

"Whoa, what is going on?" Mr. Diamond came into the tree house, moving over to Lex.

"She pushed me! She hates me!" He shrieked, curling into a ball.

"I don't hate you," I whimpered. Daddy came back over and pulled my face up to look at him. I wiped at the tears.

"Olivia, I know you don't hate him," he murmured.

"Yeah, you two are best friends," Mr. Diamond added, picking Lex up. "How could she hate you?"

"I'm bad," he muttered quietly. Mr. Diamond laughed, shaking his head. "Yeah I am."

"No you're not," I whispered, tearing my eyes from Daddy's to look at Lex. His cheeks were red from rubbing them, and his eyes shimmered. "You're my best friend. I couldn't hate you."

"You mean it?" he sniffled, wiping his nose on the back of his sleeve. I nodded eagerly.

"See?" Daddy smiled. "Friends like you two can't stay mad at each other." Lex and I smiled at each other, and ran to meet each other in a hug. He would always be my best friend. And if I ever forgot that, my daddy would always be there to remind me.

My mind drifted back to the present. Tears stung my eyes, but I blinked them back. The conversation had seemingly gone on without me, everyone jabbering about the coming week and our summer plans.

"Honeybee," Lex whispered, glancing down at me. "Hmm?"

"You, me, and the tree house. Tonight, eleven P.M., bring snacks and bedding. We're going to have a camp out," he said softly, smiling. I bit my lip, glancing up at him. "Come on, it'll be like old times."

"Okay." I nodded.

His whole face lit up. "Awesome."

He turned back to his food, watching and laughing at the appropriate times. Slowly, I followed his lead and let myself fall back into the glee they were all sporting on their faces and in their hearts.

Making a mental note, I reminded myself to go to the cemetery the next day and visit Dad's grave. It had been too long, and after graduating and going through so much without him, I wanted to spend a little time with him before summer left me with no free time.

"Olivia, remember when…" Mom went off on another story. I smiled and readied myself to listen to a night full of memories.

Chapter Twenty Two – You, Me, and the Tree House

I was in the process of changing into sweats and a t-shirt when something knocked against my window. I jolted, nearly falling over.

"Honeybee!" The familiar voice chimed from outside. I pulled the t-shirt over my head, moving to the window. Lex was standing on the ground below, a sleeping bag and pillow tucked under his arm. A smile spread across his soft lips.

Sighing, I opened the window. "What?"

"You've got five minutes before I come and get you," he warned, jerking his head toward the tree house.

"I'll be there in four," I promised, shutting the window. Heading downstairs, I went to grab some popcorn and cookies from the kitchen. Mom was sitting at the counter, staring into a bowl of tomato soup. "You okay?"

She looked up, her spoon clattering to the table top as it slipped from her fingers. "Olivia!" she gasped. "You startled me."

"Sorry." I stood next to her, my waist leaning against the edge of the counter. "Are you okay?" I questioned again. She didn't seem like herself, it was like something was off. I tilted my head to the side. "Mom?"

"I'm just letting the past twelve hours settle in." She smiled warmly, picking up the spoon. She stirred the soup, sending ripples through the hot liquid. "When you were born, and my mind wandered to the future, I never once thought I would be going through this alone. Your dad was always next to me, holding me as our little girl grew up."

I bit my lip, not knowing what to say. I missed my dad, but Mom missed her husband. She missed the man she fell in love with, the man she had a child with. I couldn't imagine the heartbreak she must've felt.

"He would've been so proud of you," she murmured, looking up at me. A weak smile flittered to my face. "And I'm very proud of you."

"Thanks, Mom." I pushed my glasses back up on my nose. The daze seemed to pass from her eyes, and I knew she wasn't in the past anymore, or thinking so carefully about Dad, and the life we all missed out on when that drunk driver took him away. I sighed, pushing the memories from my mind. "Lex is waiting for me to come outside."

She nodded, having been informed on the way home that he was coming over. "Are you sure you're alright with that?"

"Yeah." I nodded, not totally confident in my answer. "It'll be fine. Besides, it's not like either of us have anything else to do tonight. So it'll be nice to just hang out and stuff." Glancing at the clock, I noted that I was running out of time. "He gave me five minutes before he's coming to get me. So I'm going to go outside," I told her, picking up the snacks and kissing her cheek.

She chuckled. "Alright. Well, just be smart. I might come up there or spy on you, so be careful what you two do," she warned. I gulped, nodding. "Good. Have fun."

With the snacks, and an extra sweatshirt in my arms, I headed outside. Just as I opened the door, Lex appeared on the front porch, his hand poised to knock. I smiled triumphantly. "Ha."

He followed after me, taking the cookies from my hands and opening the package. "You're lucky I didn't have the patience to count and just guessed when the five minutes was up." He popped a cookie into his mouth, chomping obnoxiously.

"You're lucky I'm letting you come over at all, you're such an unpleasant eater." I threw the sweater around my neck, clutching the bag of popcorn tightly as I started up the ladder. If taking snacks up to the tree house wasn't a regular thing, I would've been afraid of falling flat on my back and breaking a limb or two.

Lex scoffed, probably spitting cookie crumbs all over the yard. "I am not."

When I stepped onto the floor of the tree house, I saw Lex had already made himself comfortable. The sleeping bag and blow up mattress I'd set up earlier had been shoved aside, making room for the small living room he'd brought up with him. He had his iPod and a small set of speakers, along with his laptop and a few movies. The air mattress I'd inflated and left for myself, was littered with his stuff. My sleeping bag seemed to have disappeared, and his covered the whole mattress.

"Lex," I grumbled, turning to look as he stood beside me.

"What? I'm just making it fair. You took up the whole mattress. I'm not sleeping on the floor." He set the cookies down.

"You took the whole mattress!" I hissed, glaring at him.

"I don't recall you being this selfish when we were younger," he sighed, like he was disappointed in me.

"I was naïve. Don't hold it against me," I muttered, sitting down on his sleeping bag, the mattress dipping with the added weight.

"You're still naïve," he chuckled, shaking his hair out of his eyes. "Now! What do you want to do? We obviously can't go to sleep for a while, because that's just lame." He sat down next to me, our knees touching in the close proximity.

"We could talk about our feelings, or watch movies, or stuff our faces with fattening foods," I offered up, looking around the tree house. "I'm up for whatever."

He waggled his eyes suggestively. "You need to be careful what you say." I slapped his arm, causing him to laugh. "I was kidding. How about we do a combination of all three? Eat food, purge emotion, and zone out in front of a screen?"

"Sounds like an excellent plan," I answered, opening the popcorn and taking a handful.

"Of course it's an excellent plan. I came up with it," he boasted, oozing of confidence.

"Of course," I muttered under my breath.

Lex moved to his computer, slipping a movie into it and then pressing play. He sat next to me again. The snack he'd brought consisted of crackers, Poptarts, and a box of soda cans. Ever since we were younger, we'd grown to have similar taste in snack food.

"What movie?" I asked, consuming more buttery popcorn.

"It's my favorite mov–"

"Peter Pan." I smiled at his look of annoyance.

"How did you know?"

"I do know you pretty well," I reminded him. "We pretty much grew up together, remember?"

"I didn't think you would remember," he sighed, leaning on his knees.

"Yee of little faith," I chided.

"We haven't watched it together for so long, I figured you'd think I had moved on to something more masculine."

"You? Never." I shook my head. "No movie will ever mean as much to you as this one does. Even though you have some ill-conceived hatred for Peter, you love Tinker Bell, and for some reason you can sympathize with Hook, which I don't get because he hurts her."

"I'm impressed, Bee," he said, looking back as the opening credits started. "I thought you would forget things about me."

"I'm a good friend," I chided.

"You are," he agreed, nudging my shoulder. "So, you purge your emotions first. I saw the look on your face tonight when they were talking about your dad." He looked over at me, concern welling in his irises. "Are you okay?"

I gave a humorless laugh, a sad smile pulling at my lips. "No." I pulled my knees up to my chest. "I miss him." I bit my lip. It ached from how many times I'd used it to avoid tears in the past six hours. "He was my dad. He was supposed to be there tonight and intimidate the first guy brave enough to ask me out. I feel like half my childhood is missing." I sniffled. "There were so many families there tonight, complete and happy families. But mine wasn't one of them. There's this hole in my heart, and I'll never be able to fill it."

Lex's hand found mine, clasping our fingers together. "There's nothing I can say that will make you feel better, Honeybee."

I know.

"But, that doesn't mean I won't try."

I met his gaze. I could feel myself falling into his atmosphere, being pulled closer by his gravity. My eyes closed when his forehead leaned against mine. His warm breath cascaded over my face, sending chills down my back.

"Honeybee," he murmured, his fingers gently touching my face, caressing my skin.

My heart pounded against my chest, trying to beat its way out and cuddle up next to his. "Yes?"

"I think—"

"Lex!" A loud voice hollered. We broke apart, looking wildly for the responsible party. "Lex!" The voice came again.

He stood, taking his warmth away, and moved to the door. "Dad?" he groaned, glancing back at me for a moment. "What is it?" he asked.

"I need your help. There's a leak in the garage. Don't take too much time. That's your car sitting in the garage," he warned. I heard his footsteps move away.

Lex muttered under his breath before turning back to me. "I better go help him before he gets mad." He looked torn. "I'll try to hurry and be back soon."

"Okay," I mumbled, pulling the sleeping bag around me. It was then I noticed he'd laid my sleeping bag down, unzipping it all the way and covering the mattress like a sheet, using his sleeping bag to act like a comforter. "Want me to pause the movie?"

He shook his head, pulling his shoes on. "No, that's fine. You keep watching it."

I rolled my eyes, inhaling the lingering scent on his sleeping bag. "Yeah right. I'm not watching your favorite movie without you. That's practically a crime." He smirked. "Go help your dad, I'll wait up."

He sighed. "Fine," he surrendered. "Drink some soda to try and stay awake."

I saluted. "Yes sir."

He grinned once more before disappearing down the ladder, leaving me alone with my thoughts.

Soon enough, my mind grew weary of running through the moment we had been having before Steve had interrupted us. No matter how many times I ran through it in my head, I couldn't help but feel he was about to say something important. We weren't friends in that moment, we were something more, something he was about to define. I could feel it in my soul. But chance ruined the moment.

It had been almost an hour. I was beginning to worry that something was seriously wrong. Occasionally, I would hear one of them shout something, but it was never clear enough to know what they were talking about. It was making me nervous. They were already walking on a brittle relationship. If either of them pushed too hard things could shatter.

Sighing, I slipped under the top sleeping bag, snuggling into the warmth. Yawning became more frequent, and my eyelids grew heavy. No amount of pinching my arms could wake me, though I continued to pinch myself every time I almost nodded off, anyways.

Another yell across the street confirmed they were still dealing with whatever had happened, and he likely wouldn't be back anytime soon.

"Sorry, Lex." My eyelids closed, and I let out a deep sigh, moving the pillow to support my head better. The flickering lights on the laptop were dull, fading into the darkness as sleep beckoned me.

As I drifted off, my thoughts centered on the boy I was in love with. The way he'd laughed and smiled, enjoying his time around me. The way he'd touched my hand, and promised to never stop trying. His words had been spoken in gentle love.

Ever since the camping trip, things had changed so dramatically. The idea of Lex and I being friends again was so far from a reality, that it never even crossed my mind as a possibility. But now, we were friends again. There was trust. I'd never found the idea of us becoming more than friends so realistic. Maybe not all Honeybees died after the first sting. Perhaps there were some that endured, and didn't give up hope even when there was nothing to hold onto.

The sound of someone coming up the ladder made my heart beat faster. My nerves kicked in, worrying that it wasn't Lex, but someone who was going to kill me and then bury my body in six different states.

"Honeybee, did you go to sleep?" Lex whispered, bringing ease to my fears.

"Almost," I whispered, too weary to turn over and look at him. "Everything okay?"

"Yeah," he murmured. The mattress moved as he slid on next to me. The cold night air held onto his skin. I shivered when he moved a little too close. "Want to keep watching the movie?"

"I'm going to fall asleep," I told him, my words barely above a whisper.

"Slacker," he laughed. He poked my shoulder. When I didn't move, he slid up right next to me, his body cold against mine. "Why are you so sleepy?"

"It's been a long day," I answered, sighing and turning to face him. We were inches apart.

"No excuse." His eyes twinkled. "You said you would stay up with me and watch the movie. That's what we're going to do."

"I'm going to fall asleep," I repeated, yawning through my words. My eyelids closed. I jerked when a cold hand pressed against my neck, his thumb brushed along my jaw. "Lex!"

"Come on, this is our first night as high school graduates. We can't waste it sleeping."

"I can." I pulled the top sleeping bag closer to me, trying to ward off some of his chill.

"Please?" he whispered. When my eyes blinked open, I saw the puppy dog look on his face, his lip jutting out in a pout. I didn't know how he could make that look attractive, but he did.

"Fine," I sighed, trying to sit up more. He smiled brightly and pushed play, sitting close to me. I leaned against his shoulder, trying to stay awake. He pulled the sleeping bag around us, his head resting against mine. A small smile found its way to my face. "Is this a better way to celebrate?"

"Of course," he replied brightly. "And this isn't a onetime deal. Prepare yourself, Honeybee." His eyes danced with excitement, transferring the giddy feeling to me.

"Prepare myself?" Butterflies danced in my stomach.

He nodded, running his fingers up my arm, twisting the ends of my hair around. "Yes, prepare."

"Why?" I asked, breathlessly.

Lex let his eyes trail over my face, seemingly taking in as many details as he could. Slowly, a playful smile stretched across the lips I couldn't get out of my head.

"The summer is just beginning."

About the author

Caity's love of writing started in the eighth grade. From there she has continued to write more and try to better her skills. Hello, Honeybee was the first work that she completed. It also became a top rated story on Inkpop.com. This achievement came with a review from Harper Collins. Caity has finished two more books since Hello, Honeybee, and plans to publish them.

Lex and Honeybee will be back soon, in
"Hello, Handsome"

Made in the USA
Charleston, SC
22 June 2013